THE ETERNAL CHAOS OF LOVE

PORCHES

Contents

Contents

Foreword

It is truly crazy how people you have never met in person your life become a huge part of you and your creative process. It is not every day your best friend gets to publish a book and find a creative outlet. Porches' drive and imagination knows no bounds. He wrote this book at a time when everything exactly was not hunky dory in his life. He challenged all his thoughts and translated it into something positive, enriching, and authentic.

He wanted to put out something good out in the world and it makes me glad to see it happen. There are a lot of things that makes me want to continue my friendship with him and what makes him unique as an author is that he is driven, passionate, and judges everything with honesty. I was surprised at the pace with which he finished his book.

One could say he has left a piece of his heart in this book. So, when you read this book today, I hope you see his vision. I hope you see an author who has spent most of his life living on stories from around the world that kept him going. I hope you see why Porches can carve out a splendid piece of work.

Love,
Jacqueline J

Note From The Author

Dear Reader

First up, I sincerely thank you for choosing this book and giving your precious time to read this.

This is my first novel, a simple world I created here is set in Tamil Nadu and Pondicherry. I have always fascinated by the discrete geographic and diverse anthropology of Tamil Nadu. This entire story will take you through the beaches, a pilgrimage island, the rich heritage of western ghats and some parts of Pondicherry too.

Fictions are always blended with truths, here I have taken the fictional liberty as a licence to blend it with the historical moments and places. In case if you find any mistake or inappropriate to the history and to the true nature of the place, kindly apologize. Even though the story set in Tamil speaking region of the country, all the characters' conversations are narrated in English only, and now I kindly ask again to apologize me if you find mistakes in my English.

Ideologies may vary, you may disagree with the direction where the characters lead to but what stays eternal throughout the journey is love and love only. "Love" and "Chaos" are tangential points, they always share moments together. Only thing that lasts long is love. Every character in this story is somehow coupled with love in any form. I hope you too believe love is the driving force of one's life, which I strongly believe in. To love and to be loved is the basic thing every human needs.

Right from the big bang, everything in the universe is processed by a theory called, Chaos theory. It states that, there are underlying patterns, interconnection, constant feedback loops, repetition, self-similarity, fractals, and self-organization.

This story passes through both good and evil of our society. As we all know our society is compiled with both goodness and evilness, and when it meets the innocence and love, the respective result is something unimaginable. Loneliness and love share great bond together, they are hard to separate. But only thing that kills loneliness is love and the only thing that kills love is loneliness.

I have narrated the incidents that happens to be the derivates of chaos theory in the summer of the year 2013. Story revolves around mainly three characters, a teen girl from Rameswaram, a man in twenties from Chennai, and an old man from Western ghats. Series of incidents that occurs within few days lead to the solution of few problems.

This is a work of fiction. Any names or characters, businesses or places, events, or incidents, are fictitious. Any resemblance to actual persons, living or dead, or actual events is purely coincidental. I am not intended to hurt the sentiments of any individual, community, or religion.

Kindly asking you to take a deep breath and travel back with me to 2013 and please be ready to travel with the flow like air, but with the path and destiny like a river. Hope you enjoy it!

Lots of love and gratitude
Porches

To my Parents
To the Universe
To the Chaos theory
To Charlie Chaplin
To Paulo Coelho

CHAPTER ONE

On a full moon day's early morning in April 2013 a young girl who is at the age of seventeen, a typical brown South Indian Islamic girl with hijab scarf around head and neck rushes onto the terrace with her mobile and switched it on. She texted him a paragraph with those very lesser SMS balance she had at that time. He did not respond quickly as time is already half past three. Cool breeze from the sea started to brush her brains through her ears as her home is just under one kilometre from the Palk strait in the north and around six kilometres to the Gulf of Mannar in south, as her home lies in a tiny island called Rameswaram. Ocean waves has got no job particularly in this island due to the very shallow water level but the water body get itself shined and glowing under the moon, we might call it as a party nights of large water bodies that divide continents.

She might able to see some her beloved friend Bay of Bengal just after a small walk to enjoy the nature's own party and can submit our presence to bale dance of the world's beautiful couples "Ocean and Moon" but she sat at the corner of the terrace where she used to read for her twelfth board exams just a month ago, the famous TV tower light and the light house's rotation of lights usually hits their terrace regularly.

So many moments flashed in her mind right from her early love days to the last few days of her school life, everything seemed like a mirage to her now.

She thinks and asks "Why would you do this to me? I never known I would sit like a waste piece of paper in an early morning like this and regret about what has happened with you?".

Tears started to flow down as she hazed the stars above which reminded her of the good old love days with her boyfriend but somehow, she refuses her eyes to look at the full and bright moon on that special to our lunar planet, she never thought that this beautiful place of heaven would turn into the place of spending the darkest phase and time of her life.

She had the valid reason that she stopped herself from watching the moon as per as her family's religious beliefs has concerned, they use to give a sight at moon with very ethnic religious cause, which makes her bit guilty as that remind her of her very own father. She is the only daughter of her father Abdul Waqar a fifty-five-year-old small profit businessman in the town. He runs an electronic goods shop in the town part of Rameswaram an island town located down south of India in a district named Ramanathapuram but mostly the people will identify Rameswaram not from the Indian political map but from the mythical map of Ramayana, or we simply call it as the land which is just about to connect India with Sri Lanka but somehow managed to miss it for a cause.

Abdul Waqar wants her daughter to be a queen of Rameswaram so he wanted to name her "Shazana" means the princess or the daughter of a king according to the Holy Quran but her mother Khadija saw her child as a gift of Allah which indicates an another name from the Holy Quran "Shiza" both were confused at that time and starts arguing between themselves suddenly a sparkling laughter sound comes from cradle they both came to witness the glittering and glow from the face of her new born daughter at that point both came to a conclusion that they should be naming their daughter "Sana Amyra" meaning the glittering princess according to the Holy Quran ! Really a holy laugh that one.

But seventeen years and on with five feet and six inch taller in the same house, Sana who was named after her glittering smile and glowing graceful face is not seems to be that happy and left stranded from someone she loved. Her house is a single storey building which made her to think about falling but her biological sense itched her brain as that will not be a good idea to live with a broken hand or leg which is even tough to elope from the house. Now as the time Sana does stir all these thoughts in her tiny dual braid which her mom tied in the evening under her hijab.

The time is now quarter to five and she hears her father's morning prayer. Sana is now hesitant to go downstairs as her father might ask something about her early wake up as she is a poor liar. So, she decided to stay up.

Now she again texted him saying "I don't think I'll survive with this; I feel like I'm left alone how can you sleep peacefully? Please come to my home today please talk with my dad pleaseee I beg you". It took almost ten minutes for Sana to type this text and then she cried by biting her palm as it works as sound proof for crying here after crying out loud within her hands for some time she wipes her tears and looked up the sky which is now glowing graceful with glittering just like Sana smiled seventeen years ago at the cradle, due to the outcome of Sun from the eastern part of Bay of Bengal, Sana then realises it's the Dawn.

She comes down and greets her father a very happy morning in their religious way and started doing morning prayer. In fact, for her father's sake. Adding to the fact that Sana is not that religious person comparing to the others in her family.

Sana's home consists of four members Sana's father Abdul Waqar her mother Khadija Begum and her grandmother Aisha Biwi, the mother of Waqar.

Everyone in her home is purely religious and follows almost every Islamic tradition without fail but their Hajj pilgrimage tour is yet to be fulfilled as Waqar has some debts to be paid which was bought for the educational expenses of Sana. All the family members had the breakfast and Waqar is getting ready to open his shop "Sana electronics".

He uses to go with that old scooter which needs to be kicked hard to get started. Sana was cleaning the vessels after breakfast and taking the regular pills for her grandmother with bearing the sleepless overnight's hangover. As she approached her grandmother to give her pills, immediately she fainted down and Aisha the grandmother who is almost going to hit century by next year screams like Vera Miles from Alfred Hitchcock's nineteen sixty Psycho movie.

***

Few days after to that morning, when all these flurries are happening at Rameswaram, one of the signals at the hot place of Chennai a traffic chaos arises courtesy of an unmoved car that did not follow the green signal. It was almost nine in the morning all office workers and people who are about to start their day have stranded due to this traffic chaos made by this unmoved car.

Many came up to the car and shocked to see the driver seat. A young tall and half fit brown man with sharp nose and pretty fleshy eyes around twenty-three sleeping by holding the steering and he wakes up from the noise created by the people, he soon starts the car and clears the way and realises about the mess he created in quite few minutes.

It was a heavy night shift for him, he cannot handle the sudden rotation of shift which suddenly changed his sleep cycle so as the result of that, he fell asleep right at the signal with the help of the red signal's one hundred- and fourteen-seconds countdown. He rushed his car to the nearby tea shop and buys a cigarette. As he emits the smoke, he receives a call from his friend, he attends to listens

"Hey Gautam you still got to have another client to clear the tally can you please log into your mail when you reach your home", friend speaks over the phone.

“What the hell, see! I have worked for twelve hours without a sleep man; I can't just get carried away with the work! I have my body to care and mind doesn't bend as per your convenience" Gautam replies.

Gautam is a typical software developer whom receives a better package than that of his college mates who were slated to join software testing instead of developing but Gautam had other ideas as he always thinks ahead and has good analytical skills which bringing him a work to do and money to feed himself.

His parents are yet to divorce, Father Ezhil Arasan lies in Hyderabad; who works in a multinational marketing agency and Mother Vaithegi stays at Bangalore; who works as an assistant professor in an Engineering college and the author of many solution books for Engineering Entrance Exams. His mother lives with one disappointment with her son as he is not the one among the lakhs to be benefited by her entrance exam books but Gautam is still an Engineer though, who got selected in a college by attending Tamil Nadu Engineering Counselling but that does not, please his mother either so both stopped talking frequently as he's not seemingly a mom's boy. She always had one belief that problem solving in mathematics is easy than parenting so she decided to involve herself into the problem making that is setting up question papers for entrance exam and creating scenario's that can be possibly solved using mathematical functions.

Money is not the problem for Gautam as he works in a reputed software company but the mental illness level raises day by day like the Antarctic continent's sea level, this phone call adds extra one milli meter rise in the stress and he asks over the phone "Can you please allot someone?".

His friend replies "That's not the case here it's your work and you got to have a finishing kick here man come on".

Gautam almost fed up with this work but he needs money to survive, he started hating his parents that is why he moved away from the city to find himself close to the beach. He cuts the call and at that time the cigarette ends and he starts the car. As reaching home, all the tiredness in the world invited him with smile with clueless state of mind, he smiled back at it.

He is staying alone in a two BHK apartment with a balcony which gives a great glance at the very much busy roads of OMR. He is now a single to say in relationship but he had a girlfriend and who seem like a good old friend now, who meets at a bay bar and shares lemonade the last message from her to him was her marriage invitation in fact which Gautam showed up with fifteen thousand worth blazers just to show off that no one asked for.

Now after brushing the teeth Gautam did not find anything to eat for breakfast as the sleep would be the best recipe to him as of now but the key has triggered from his office so he must resume the work so he freshens up and looks all set to work then he opens the laptop and connects it to the modem he bought three months ago.

By the time the laptop connects to the network he rests his neck back to sofa giving a glance to the plain ceiling with a fan running at the medium speed his mind flashes many moments right from his parents broke up with their relationship when he was five which is the first instance of him being mentally disturbed he also reminds of the day when he was watching his favourite cartoon at evening very interestingly suddenly his mom dragged him and took him away from the house fighting with his father and he still tries to figure out what might have happened on that day which even he asked his mother but she forgot the real cause.

Next stop was the adolescent behaviours that caused him so many troubles, the teenage friendship seemed not that sweet for him the memories of his teenage also happens to be the one to forget. As he thinks these many memories through his mind, he also reminds his college love who is his ex-girlfriend now, but he opens his eyes suddenly scratches it and logs into his work. He cannot quietly figure out who made the mess of the problem that arose suddenly last night in the office which is the cause of his overtime duty now, he seems frustrated and yells at his colleagues as he is now in a lunatic phase without sleep and working continuously for twenty hours now but one of his project heads just mailed him "Gautam! You are paid for what you do please stay within your limits and finish this off soon it's almost eleven o clock in the morning! Do you know what time it is now in United States? Client is patiently waiting online please clarify cheers".

On seeing this pretty long greeted message from one of his project head Gautam's eye balls started rolling and also it attains the state of sunset scenario inside the eyes it has got too red but he has got no chill this time he immediately closes the laptop and lied down on the table.

Gautam closes his eyes after a long run of twenty hours or so.

***

At Rameswaram, present day, Sana opens her eyes to find herself lying at the hospital, third bottle of glucose is about to end. She finds no one other than one nurse inside the room.

Sana calls her and asks "Where are my parents?". Nurse shocks and hesitantly opens the door and calls her parents suddenly her parents Waqar and Khadija rushed into the room and saw her, Waqar stood aside and looked shaken by something Khadija came to her and starts crying and beating her daughter who is having a sip of glucose through IV.

Sana had no idea why her mother is beating and crying, suddenly the nurse came and cleared the parents from the room, then closed the door to change the glucose bottle, Sana thinks that something has been found by her parents but not sure is that the one why her mother beaten her but just to clarify the fact she hesitantly asks the nurse "Sister, does my parents know that I'm pregnant?". Nurse replied "Yes".

CHAPTER TWO

The shock wave spread all over Rameswaram, but that is not a recent shock for Sana as she had known this a week ago. Doctors reported that Sana is now two months pregnant. Both Waqar and Khadija were sitting on the bench in each end of the bench looks stunned in the corridor of hospital right out of Sana's ward. The corridor is filled by several people like a man calling over phone to his friend about his newly born daughter and the other one who seems so happy that his brother's operation was successful and he will be able to walk after two years and then a man who is selling tea inside hospital.

Seeing all these happy moments, the tea seller just came near Waqar and asks for a tea which Waqar ignored and the he passes onto Khadija who is busy cleaning her nose after two hours of continues crying. He offers a cup of tea to her but Khadija did not bat an eye at him and then he says "Just enjoy the moment madam your daughter is now a blessed girl as she gave to another precious girl to this world! So have a nice cup of tea now" now he moves back to Waqar and says "Bhai be happy and enjoy this moment Allah has always blessed you."

After hearing this Waqar gets up and started walking away which made Khadija to follow him as well, she rushed to him and asked "What are we going to do?"

"We must kill her or kill ourselves" Waqar replied.

Khadija wants her daughter to come home first as she wanted this news must not spread among their relatives so both Waqar and Khadija has decided to ask doctor to discharge herself as early as possible, coincidently chief doctor arrived and asks Sana to take rest at home. Both Waqar and Khadija who were waiting outside rushed to pay the bills and make the things ready to take her back home, Waqar first pays the bill and followed by Khadija hires the auto rickshaw to home, all of these happened in a flash. Sana feels highly embraced to go back to home and meet her parents in straight again to talk about her pregnancy and stuffs, but she has no other chance as of now.

Waqar did not bought any medicines as prescribed which is mandatory process after consulting the doctor, he wanted to leave the place and do not want to be witnessed by someone he knows. As she was discharged Sana wants her hijab back to wear it, nurse gave it to her Sana wears her hijab fully covered and Khadija gave a rave look at her and both leaves that place.

In the autorickshaw Waqar occupies a place in front besides the driver and both Khadija and Sana have taken the back seats, Khadija is so furious to yell at her daughter and Waqar eventually calms her down. They reached home Sana stared crying and Khadija stops her as she did not want her to cry outside home and make it as a serious issue.

As the door opened Khadija starts beating her and immediately Waqar locked the door and stares at Sana, suddenly Sana fell on the knees and starts crying.

Life at stake for Sana! Parents can go any extreme to save their pride, but their religion does not support any immoral activities like that, and also suicide is not permitted in Islam.

After sometime the entire home sounds like a "calm after storm" courtesy of crying from both Khadija and Sana Waqar approached his daughter to speak some words, Waqar has a serious belief in his religion which Sana lacked even though she is her father's little and only princess. Waqar has always been disappointed with the fact that Sana does not practices serious Islam.

Waqar asks Sana "tell me who is the reason behind it, do not get embraced here after we should solve it, please co-operate with me! See your mom is upset and you are crying like a hell I do not want our home is to be like this".

Sana slowly looks at her father's face and she wanted to hug her father but something hesitates and starts crying again with head and hands bend towards him. Waqar took her daughter and cleared her face with water and gave his mobile and asks her to call him. Sana shocked for a moment so does is Khadija, immediately Sana calls his boyfriend to whom she texted back in the early morning which she did not received a single reply even. Now she is calling from his father's phone number which is unknown to his boyfriend.

Phone ring once the twice then thrice and rings on and on he finally picks up the call and says "hello" Sana replied in excitement "Hey this is me Sana" she cries and then says "Please come home and talk to my parents they know everything."

He then replies "Sana, I cannot repeatedly tell you this every time! Understand that was an accident I cannot come and marry you please abort it and move on with your life and please do not call me again we're done! Take care"

Sana stunned and Waqar slowly takes his phone from her hand and sees Khadija, whom also looks like lost everything.

Waqar tells Khadija "This is not our daughter's fault! It is Djinn game it has possessed our girl" as he says Khadija closes her mouth with fear, Sana looking at her father with some sort of panic but she did not have a clue for what is going to happen for her next.

***

Waking up after a nap of 2 hours Gautam realises that he has messed up a bit of things in his office, he has a habit of food ordering very often whenever he feels anything odd, he will be ordering food anyway anytime irrespective of his hungriness. Room is mostly filled with empty beer bottles, food wrappers and unwashed cloths.

He opens his mobile to call his favourite fast-food restaurant something suddenly an advertisement pops up in his new model android phone showing "Rent a Resort", he notes down the apps name in his mind and closes it then he orders a cold coffee with two crispy burgers alongside a carbonated soft drink.4

In the meantime, he went to the balcony in his flat and does a push ups workout he receives a call and he attends "Hey Gautam! It is time and you have to listen what I'm going to say please join the meeting at six in the evening hope you aware of the situation right now" His manager speaks over phone.

Gautam again receives a call but this is from the food delivery partner. Gautam picks his order and gave a glance at his phone again, now again the advertisement "Rent a Resort" pops up, he opens and he registered his details in it. In few minutes he receives a call from an unknown number that says "Hello Gautam! We are calling from rent a resort Pondicherry hope you are having a good day" a female voice spoke with that typical dramatic voice tone people at help desks have, Gautam who is going through a tough and hard unable to answer for the "Hope you're having a good day?" question but managed to answer politely and came to know about the place. Female voice then said "Our company "Forest Fossils" has so many projects like this! rent a resort offer valid until this month's end you will be paying twenty-four thousand and four hundred and ninety-nine only to rent a resort for a day and you can enjoy your peaceful time alone."

Gautam rubs his eyes and says "Hello I am already alone I live in my flat without anyone, so can you please provide me place where there are lot of people? Can you?"

After asking Gautam finishes his food and approaches to wash his hands and plate kept his phone aside but that female voices keep talking about the plans and offers, as he returns to pick his phone she is saying "Just like you rent a resort, you can also rent a car rent or a restaurant or rent a pool whatever you want you can have".

Gautam in reply says "Shall we rent people?" the female voice shocked and asks "What?"

"Hmm yeah! I am in need of people people's love in fact people's presence is so precious for me it feels so essential to me, rather than being in a world filled with binary and surrounded by computer languages I would like to meet or be with someone doesn't possess binary and speaks the language the warmth knows! I need people."

As Gautam says this there is an awkward silence maintained through the phone call by that lady voice then she replied "Sorry sir currently we're not providing such services hope you liked our experience and have a good day sir thank you".

Call ends, Gautam closes his eyes to recollect the memories that he had when he was surrounded by some amount of people to make fun and at least to be with, but all those things soon vanished, he feels so lonely now and like adding insult to the injury his job also makes his mind a best garbage in the town. He also had plans to leave the job and roam around the world but the money factor which is the most essential factor to survive in this world stopped to take that decision and also, he had plans to elope from the scenes but some sophistication he feels stopped him. Gautam still not opened his eyes thinking about every single trauma he faced. He wanted to go somewhere, he needs people to talk about, how the absence of certain people hurt him and why he is so urge in need of people.

Need of people and their absence is the most liked twin thing of this human's known universe, it can leave people alone and it will squeeze one's heart like a sponge to push to an extreme, which a mind can go.

Sun starts to show the orange rays to indicate that it is going to take rest and his fellow partner moon will take over the "celestial hope" duty.

CHAPTER THREE

Few evenings prior to when Gautam had that twenty-four-hours marathon work, as the dusk appears on the sky the most beautiful twilight part of the day begins in Ooty, a hill region in Tamil Nadu almost four hundred kilometres away from Chennai. Glenmorgan a small village in the Ooty hills which has a special dam reservoir and an age-old tea estate is also located at this place. This place is mostly landslide prone zone as it is geographically located on the slides of the Glenmorgan valley.

Glenmorgan has several habitations besides the very small tea estate, people who works there and people who worked there in the past along with the family resides in a street which was named after Sir Alister Wood a former British officer who was part of this estate's foundation and. He played an important role in saving lives in 1949's landslides. The main occupation of the people of the street is tea leave cultivation in the very small tea estate area. They make trade with many popular tea brands.

In that street, a sixty-six-year-old man whose name is Paul, he looks so old, has grey silver hairs, pure white beard and has a non-Indian English skin tone, working as a milk man in the morning and food delivery man in the night, Sir Alister Wood Street geographically located on the lowest part of Glenmorgan village hence in need of the vegetable, poultry, and the dairy products they need to climb up a small hill to get those. So, the old man has appointed himself to do the job as he knowns every single path to climb the forest even at dark night.

He uses travel with a back bag with consists of empty milk bottles with names in scripted for better recognition and also, he carries small bundle packs of chilli powder to tackle animals that comes in his way he even tackled and managed to escape from a tiger many years ago.

That evening was so dark, an early sunset created a haunting experience for Paul as he heads back home after buying vegetables for a family in his street, Paul has not learned about the usage of mobile phone, and he also didn't care about that since that place is a remote area and its uncared by the government and even NGOs. He thinks about his wife, who is down there in his house. As it is getting late, he worries about his wife in mind, that whether she has taken her medicines or not. Paul thinks, Mrs. Paul has a habit of eating dinner only with Paul she never missed the supper with her husband that day also she seems waiting for her husband to come home for dinner.

It was fully dark and almost every possible light has gone down Paul seems struggling to find his way in that dark time, he also getting frustrated as he cannot call his wife and warn her to have her pressure tablets as soon as possible. Somehow, he reaches down at almost eight in the night he approaches to the clay house which has the elephant drawing, which denotes a mother elephant saves its calf from a tree falling with its tusk made on the wall from where they ordered the vegetables. Paul is fully wet yet he covered all the vegetables with the woollen cloth. He delivers the vegetables and asks for a piece of carrot from the package he bought, he added "It was so pure and fresh I wanted to buy some for my wife but it started to become dark and she'll be alone here so can you lend me a carrot?" Young man from the house gives the carrot. Paul received a carrot and rushes back to his home. He enters the home with slight hesitation as his wife is going to yell at him for returning so late.

Mrs. Paul came from the kitchen with the candle as the power was shut due to rain, she placed the candle and greeted her husband with angry face.

Mrs. Paul said "It has been a while since you were this late! So, you started this practice again uh?"

Paul replied, "No, but I have a reason to be this late."

"I know the reason, the friend of yours, that old man from Glenmorgan reservoir dam, damn! You started to hang around like teens, right?" asked Mrs. Paul.

Paul with that shaky voice designated to the old people says "No, definitely not today, I know you must be angry but you might have seen the climate played a role here, it's so cold, rain starts to pour heavily I can't run into the woods up there you see I'm not twenty-six, I'm sixty-six now so that means you're sixty-three" as he says this Mrs. Paul stops him with a stare as she does not want him to mention her old age now.

Immediately Paul shows the carrot he bought and gave it so hesitantly to her she takes that in hand and bites it without telling anything. Paul's face slowly goes down as his mission of love seems impossible now, suddenly he feels something in his head which is his wife wipes his head with the towel by scolding him by saying "Don't you have any place to hide? Are you a kid? You are turning into an insane human being I ever came across."

Paul under the towel smiles and senses that she had cooked something for him. He makes his way to the kitchen to see his wife making some pancakes for him which is his favourite dish to have when it is raining outside, he gives a look at her wife who intentionally avoid the eye contact with him with her very own blush. She turns away to see the wall being painted with her portraits which was done by Paul.

Paul is an artist too; he learned the drawing art at the time he was working at the tea estate as a child. He uses to draw everything he sees on the sand and at some clay bodies, in fact he once drawn an elephant drawing on the newly built clay house which is still being a showcase. Paul actually drawn her wife's portraits on every corner of the house denoting the certain emotions for each painting right from love, lust, sweet, bitter, disgust, sad, excitement, pity and anger. The last one is the quite common though he feels, he did this not only to show his drawing talents and he also wants his wife's face to fill his walls.

As they seem busy with eye contact avoiding game the pancakes called them and both rushed into the kitchen and make pancakes, but the baking consistency of the pancake is bit low suddenly they both starts blaming each other and finally Paul overtakes her wife in argument and says "I'll make the pancakes today" then Mrs. Paul coughs just to tease him. Rain slowly stops outside and mandatory silence filled the place, still the power is shut for some safety reasons. Paul lights the fire stick to keep the place warmth and his wife joined then work in meantime Paul made three pancakes of his own.

Paul filled the fire place with sticks and paper to make sure the chimney is fully lightened up to keep the place warmth.

The hot pancakes taste extra delicious in accordance to the climate and the silence after the rainfall. The mood also swings like a pendulum for Mrs. Paul as she stopped yelling at her husband. She works on the table to make it clean and change into a better place to have a nice supper together with the candles on, Hmm! Sounds like a romantic candle light dinner, isn't it? Courtesy of power cut. It was cool even in the night of April where people at most of the other parts of the country would be dying for air-conditioned rooms to reside, but Glenmorgan offers a free indoor and outdoor air-conditioned places to live.

Mr and Mrs. Paul are not aware of, they are going to have a candle light dinner together as they just stopped a fight which seem like most of the young couples do. Paul placed the pancake in order to serve for her wife, but she is not quite satisfied with baking consistency of the pancakes Paul made. She starred at him to indicate that he has messed up the entire dinner they were about to have, but Paul somehow wanted her wife to eat the half-baked pancakes he made so he politely and quite romantically starts talking to his wife.

"Have you ever thought that you have a more caring husband who offers pancakes for you?" Paul asked.

Mrs. Paul looks at him for few seconds and replied "I never thought you would be a half-baked man just like this pancake." Paul gasps in embracement.

Paul wanted to know that how much his wife loves him because she never opened up about her love towards him in all these forty years of togetherness so he repeatedly keeps asking some questions that he wants to know, he asks "I want to ask this to you for a very long time, I know these pancake are quite bad but that we can manage by making the other ones but what I wanted to know is what made you stay with me? despite me having all these flaws and cons"

Mrs. Paul's face changed from starring at him to normally looking at him. Paul immediately puts his head down which he always does to escape from the embracement. She replied nothing but she gets up and goes to kitchen and makes flour to make the better pancakes. Paul also followed her and asks "So this is the thing, I make mistakes and I never been a good husband I never took you out of this place I never satisfied you in many aspects of life, but my question is, in all these forty years, haven't you wanted anything from me?"

In the meantime, Mrs. Paul has made a better fully baked pancakes and placed in on the table in order to serve, Paul repeatedly asks again the same question. She then took one piece of pancakes which is brown in colour, hot and super delicious. Paul sees and grabs one from her.

She then asks "Does it fully baked?" He replied "Yes"

She asks "Does it taste good?" He replied "Of course! It never tasted bad when you made these"

She replied "That's what it is, that's what the answer for your question about our life together."

Paul stopped eating and fell short of words, looks at her with eyes full of love and both stored their excess love in the eye bag they have, thanks to their age mid-sixties. Both shares a lighter moment almost after some years and both wanted to share some more time together too. Paul resumed his questioning session and starts with the most controversial and emotional question ever, he asked "Do you feel that we don't have kids?". She changed the face from normally looking to starring that she does not want to go back to their honey moon days again. Paul suddenly realised and understood the real meaning of that stare and says "No! not in that sense I asked we should have got someone to feed us and someone to take care of us and someone after us may be this is it with Mr and Mrs. Paul! Do not know why God stopped the legacy of Paul". She immediately stopped him and says "Because the God don't want to produce another retard like you!" Paul fasciately looks at her and smiles a bit which produces a cough. Mrs. Paul the washes the plates and sets up the blanket to sleep. Usually both sleeps separately in various places but that night Paul wants to sleep besides his wife.

She spreads the blanket and placed in at the place where she uses to sleep but she looks confused as Paul is already lying in that place. Paul opened his arms and said "It is so cool and still I sense some hotness dearest."

Mrs. Paul closes her mouth with her hands and again gives her trademark star at him but this time with some words "Mr. Paul we are sixty-six and not twenty-six! Am I right?" Paul replied "Yes that is what I meant we are sixty-six and not twenty-six we do not have much time relish our love and wishes so better we do all before we leave! Am I right?" Mrs. Paul again shocked and amused by the new age activities if his husband and delivers an emotion which is more of a new one which Paul did not draw in their house wall, it is the mixture of kidding smile and pretty innocent shyness the woman traditionally has in this part of the world.

Paul wanted her to hug him and tell stories about her wish and rest of life, Mrs. Paul hesitated first and then she sat down beside him, the coolest temperature just turned hot for both as they both senses the unreal beautiful warmth of their very own loving partner, that too after some time or after a bit of gap? May be.

A gap of years; a gap of decades; a gap of ages; but everything shattered within one tight hug they attained just now.

CHAPTER FOUR

Sana's home was filled with some religious essence on that day, her father actually arranged for a Godman to do some black magics to eradicate the djinn creature that possessed her daughter according to their belief. Sana seems not okay with all these stuffs as the seventeen-year-old now only cares about her child which has no father socially now.

That morning Abdul Waqar and Khadija woke up early and cleaned their house in an unusual way and Sana who have not got any of good sleeps in recent past also joined the work but her mother stopped and asked her to go inside and get ready for the prayer. The entire house looks so different and filled with some screens and wall cloths hanged here and there with some Arabic inscriptions, Aisha the grandmother of Sana just called Khadija to have some water, Sana who stood nearer to Aisha's room reacted quickly and goes to kitchen to bring some water but Aisha closed her eyes and starts murmuring some verses from Holy Quran.

Aisha completely believes that her granddaughter has been possessed by some evil force that made her to fell into the trap of the boy who made her pregnant. Khadija acted quickly and silenced Aisha and gave her some water suddenly a car approaches and parks at their gate, two men carrying a bag came into the house with some slogans and discussed some stuffs with Waqar who looks tensed. The older one among the two asks Waqar about her daughter and that made Waqar to turn at Khadija to ask about Sana and that turned Khadija to yell vigorously towards Sana who is yet to take bath just because she wanted to offer some water for her grandmother. Now Khadija immediately wants Sana to take bath and get ready for what is going to happen next. Aisha who just finished her water tries not to look at Sana and looking for every chance of avoiding eye contact with her granddaughter whom she believes as possessed.

Sana seems completely frustrated of what is happening around her and she leaks some tears and went to bath, while bathing she hears some weird noises from Aisha as she was the one who injected this Djinn concept to Waqar, which is one of the most terrifying satanic concepts of Islam. Sana who is not an ardent Islamic follower hates these types of fantasies but has a namesake faith in God only. Sana from bathroom listens these sounds and sees her belly and started talking to her two-month-old baby through mind, Sana's mind now offers no patience as she is in a state of confusion whether to abort her child or to give birth. She thinks about her lost love moments and, she touches the place which is cause of baby and feels guilty about being a sinner among her society but her better mind stopped it from thinking it and consoled herself not to think about the guilt. As the summer morning seems too bright in that tiny island town, circumstances at Sana's home seems like a climax from a Hollywood horror movie.

Two Islamic priest are sitting in order to investigate Sana and she was made to sit in a designated place, The younger one among the two priests started asking Sana, "Where did you come from?"

Sana looks clueless and said nothing

He again asked the same which Sana did the same.

The older priest opened his bag and takes out a whip starts beating Sana. She immediately falls and within the time she realises what is happening another blow falls on her back. Khadija closes her eyes with pain and Aisha now turned her eyes back at Sana which was not intended to see Sana's eyes earlier now the old lady has bought some inspirational courage from the two heavy blows of the priests. Waqar watching all these from the corner of the house has no words to say but all he wants is her daughter to be saved from the evil thing he believes.

Sana cannot bear the pain and starts crying heavily by holding her abdomen. Waqar also tries to close his eyes but just at that moment the younger priest calls him and asks him to hold Sana's shoulders. Waqar came and hold his daughter's shoulder and Sana looks at her father's face from the angle which she can see only upside down. Sana's eyes spoke and pleaded to her father to leave her and save her child. This moment the third blow falls on Sana but this time not on back, the older priest said some holy words and starts beating her on the fifth blow Sana eventually fainted, she closed her eyes by looking at her father's face from that upside down angle. Aisha prayed and Khadija opened her eyes finally which made the stored tears broke down like a dam luckily, she did not watch her daughter getting banged in the lap of her husband. Priests packed their belongings and gave Waqar a water bottle with some rose petals in it, they asked him to give that Sana on daily basis until the next rituals just like now happened which is fourteen days later to this. After the priests left the place Waqar and Khadija took Sana to her bed and made her sleep.

When Sana's favourite time of the day the evening arrives, she woke up and she cannot turn to her left as she feels some niggle on that part of her body, she slowly wakes up and notices the time. Immediately, Waqar enter her room suddenly Sana tried to cover her head and neck with hijab but then realised she is not wearing one. Waqar dragged a chair and sat nearby his daughter and asks "Is that too painful? I do not know what Allah thinks of our family". Sana replied nothing.

Waqar tells her daughter not to worry that the prayers and the rituals from the priest will help "In sha Allah nothing happens". Sana breaks down on seeing her father says "In sha Allah" as he says mostly whenever he gives support and Sana says "Life is full of so many desires at six months your mother's milk fascinates you, At five anything comes on cartoon that fascinates you, At ten anything that you learn at school fascinates you but after thirteen the teenage phase of life, everything you see fascinates and tiggers you, everything would be looking pure and shining, everything seems so new sometimes the new ones seduce us to touch and the touch actually may hurt us and they may destroy us". Waqar looks so confused and he tells "Bismillahi Rahmanirr Rahim" and then he gave the water with rose petals which priests gave him. Sana drinks a sip of water and wipes her chin. Waqar bought the bottle and asks "Dear, Father wants to ask you something, just clear me the doubt that's enough". Sana looking at her father with no clue.

Waqar asked "That boy you loved is a Muslim only, right?"

Sana looks at her father without any emotion.

CHAPTER FIVE

That was so hard down south but in the north the capital city was ready to see a man who is going to call his parents in a conference call, whom are yet to divorce. He packed things up in a hard case and he made himself ready to tour, in fact he blocked his manager and ready to abscond from his company leaving all his provident fund and contribution for insurance as he feels mind is more important than money right now.

He calls his mother and he also added his father in the call. He says 'hello happy to have you both on a single line I meant the phone call line, I've decided something, I'm leaving the job not even completed the paper works but just I need to go I need something I offers personally because everything else has been offered either by you or you" he sobs after saying this.

His mom replies "you haven't listened to my words ever since you think that you've become a man but you're not I have nothing to deal with your life happenings I love you to be a man not a coward who run away from problems".

Gautam closed his eyes and simultaneously sits down in his couch and says "Ma, you are right ma I'm a coward, but not so good as you both I hope I meant it right!"

His father then speaks a word for the first time in this entire conversation he says "Okay you are not a coward I agree but you need to be a man at least, right? What stops you being?"

Gautam now stood up and runs his eyes and speaks "Pa, how long we men fake ourselves not to cry and emote our feeling? We also have feelings to share and some stories to tell, yes pa men do cry and men do fear for things and yes men do breakdown for moments and yeah, I need some time to cherish what I have got in fact I need to live what I have missed right from my childhood."

As he says this his father cuts the call just after saying "Take yourself care then."

His mom hung up the call and she wanted him to continue his job and not to leave but she did not want to tell his son to make decisions and she is so strong in that after the decision about his college back then.

So, she told nothing but a wish she made with beautiful words like "Stay healthy". But deep inside Gautam wanted himself at the place of love peace and care that is why rented the resort few minutes ago. He packed a big bag and almost cleaned the house. He decided that he will be going on East Coast Road to Pondicherry, so he wants to go to Chennai Mofussil Bus Terminus (CMBT) of Chennai, as he do not want to catch the crowded bus from Thiruvanmiyur.

* * *

After really a long romantic night Paul woke up in the morning to do his routine services for the Glenmorgan village, he regularly serves milk for a tea shop named "James tea stall". This tea stall is maintained by the family to whom Paul delivered vegetables and milk last night. James tea stall family consists of three the man Henry Nicholas, his wife Mary Jesnitha and their seven months old boy Harris.

The entire Alister Wood street depends on Paul's grocery deliveries as most of the families there depends on the daily wages of work at estate and chocolate factory nearby by so the people cannot climb up and buy things to live in between their busy work schedule.

Paul's work has been vital for people at Glenmorgan especially at Alister Wood Street.

On that morning he meets Henry and told him about the good conversation he had last night with his wife. Henry listened the entire thing and asked "Okay! Over? Shall I get back to my work?"

Then Paul asked him back about the quality of the milk he gave last night now Henry's face enlightened and said "That was top notch I don't know how you extract such milk in that darkness loaded hills up there, you're a magician Uncle Paul". Immediately Paul started back the story about last night he also tried to talk about the pan cake incident which made them to hug but Henry stopped him an says "Uncle Paul, I have heard this million times I know she made pan cakes better than you right? And the you both talked about your old gold days"

Paul smiles and says "Yeah it was better than the other day the rain gods have helped in good way, but not much for today as she is bit angry than yesterday"

Henry says "Uncle Paul, the episode is over now we should work."

Both reached "James tea stall" and Henry started preparing his daily works and to get prepared for business. Paul used to stay there until noon and will resume his climbing up duty further. Paul and Henry's father James are childhood friends, James died fourteen years ago and after that Henry took charge of the tea stall.

Henry's family knows everything about Paul and his works, before the death of James, he offered the one share of his tea stall with Paul, but Paul refused it fully and gave that share to James' son Henry. This made Henry to love him more than he used to love he in fact requested Paul not climb up Glenmorgan, but Paul refused and said "I work for my food, everyone has their own right to work and feed themselves, I'll work until I die." And, the fact James and Paul used to be best mates as they known each other right from when they were two years old. They both shared the great bond.

That evening the rain was quite lower than yesterday Paul finished his daily work and received his daily earnings and started returning home while he was returning, he saw a guy who sells studs and ear rings. He stopped him and bought an ear ring for his wife. He wanted a slight change in design so that he asks that seller guy to make a change with the tool he had. Finally, he had his own lovely design in his hand. That was quite costly for Paul as he did not earn that much on that day.

Season is so adorable but the rain isn't. Glenmorgan is kind of place which is in India but seems like the place somewhere in Sweden or Scotland.

Paul entered the house, today he is quite earlier to home than yesterday. Paul closed the door and kept the ear ring on the table. Unlike yesterday he did not notice any pan cake smell today. Mrs. Paul seen sleeping with a heavy blanket on. Paul goes to her and asks about her health.

"I'm not sure I'm seeing the greater scenes here, wish I have come earlier today," said Paul.

"I'm surprised that you are home" replied Mrs Paul

Paul sees a happy painting of her wife near the kitchen, and he wanted her wife to bring that smile back.

Now slowly sky starts to cry.

The rain sound gives Paul the feeling "yesterday" as the previous day's rain time went well. He immediately asks her to stay up and he wants to repeat yesterday. But Mrs. Paul is not feeling brisk as yesterday as she fell sick, but she already made the cassava and placed it on the table.

Paul sees that one of the prominent paintings of Madeline she painted on the wall is slightly faded courtesy of the rain water and he came close to that and wipes it and unfortunately the painting erased further, Paul feels sad and tries to hide it from Madeline as she would be worries, because that was the very first painting that Paul painted of her.

Paul sees the painting getting erased further and he feels stranded.

Mrs. Paul suddenly interferes him, "Can you please have a meal and sleep" said Mrs. Paul.

Paul then, approached the table and opened the hotbox to see three cassavas and he then realises that he had bought her an ear ring which was placed nearby few moments ago. He took that and opened it grabs in his hands goes to her wife and he touches her shoulder and called "Madeleine."

Madeline Evy is the name of Mrs. Paul, he calls her with the name after quite a long time. She immediately responded and sees his face.

"I never thought this would happen," says Madeleine.

"Happen what?" Paul asks.

"No, there's something going down the wrong line" Madeline mumbled.

Paul smiled and gave the ear ring and asked her to wear it, he added "Do you remember what was the first gift I gave you back then?"

"I know, the same ring, but how did you find the exact design" Madeleine asked.

"I remember every incident that happened between us in our prime days, yeah I remember" said Paul with his trademark smile.

This started to get "heating" up yet again like last night but the health condition of Madeleine does not help in finding the love rhythm but still Paul asks her to wear those rings. Mrs. Paul wears the ring and asks Paul "May I rest on your lap".

Paul's face brightened up with enlightenment and placed her in his lap.

"Shall we rewind back our good old days? as I said I remember every moment I can tell you every moment," said Paul

She looked up and said "Go on"

Both started to rewind their good old days. Paul started "That was a pretty normal day in Pondicherry...."

CHAPTER SIX

Rose petals inside the water bottle floats like an abandoned boat floats on the sea after a storm, such that Sana's mind floats like the same abandoned boat. She does not have any options rather than syncing with rhythm of her religious belief and her father's adamant activities courtesy of her old ill grandma Aisha. After some number of vomiting sessions, Sana starts to rebuild her depression session. Her mother Khadija stopped talking to her as she is not the "virgin Sana" now.

Sana called her "Ma, please talk with me I feel so lonely something is pulling me I can't be imprisoned here."

"You're not the Sana we named, you spoiled yourself by applying dirt on you at seventeen" Khadija replied.

Sana looked clueless as she feels, she has done the mistake and she realises that she is the culprit as she lost her virginity at seventeen but deep inside, she has not found yet where the virginity lies in her body. Khadija cruelly scolding her on daily basis by saying she had become a mother of Sana at seventeen and starts leading a good life but Sana spoiled herself. At that time Sana's innocence and unaware of the facts about the so-called modern world confuses her and made her think about her mom that her mom is even not a virgin at her seventeenth but she cannot really bother about saying that to her as she is in red hot form of scolding her very own child whom she gave birth at sixteen after marrying Abdul Waqar at fifteen.

Khadija told "Haven't you thought about our ill old grandma she worked hard for our family for several years and she has stuck with our religious practices for more than eight years."

Now Sana do not want to think about her old grandma who gave early access birth to her children.

As the time passes by, Khadija reminds Sana of her routine work of having a sip of rose petal essence water. Sana enters Aisha's room and takes that water bottle. She shakes that and mixes the water bottle and shakes then water earns a whirlpool.

Meanwhile, the whirlpool kind of internal concussion attacks Waqar's mind while he is working in his shop. "Sana electronics" looked a little too busy in that evening and Waqar cannot find himself involved in business activities. He asks his worker Latif to take care of the shop and he leaves early.

Khalid Latif, who has been the most reliable worker and a caretaker of Sana since her younger days whom seems more like a brother figure to Sana who is ten years younger to him. Latif looks lean and skinny with curly hair, he works at Sana electronics right from the age of five, in fact he knows about electronics more than his boss Waqar.

He was introduced to Waqar by one of his relatives by mentioning that Latif's parents were took by a strong cyclone.

That day Latif senses something fishy with Waqar's face and activities and asks "Is everything okay with you?" Waqar then realises that he seems too strange in recent days and now he feels okay to confess with what happened to Sana. Latif understands the uncomfortable situation of Waqar and advices to close the shop early and suggests a trip to nearby shore. Waqar agreed and closes the shop and asks Latif to drive the bike to "Jadayu Teertha" which is a famous spot in Rameswaram.

It is a Hindu temple but they like the place for its surreal ambience and the sea breeze it provides, both sits there and Waqar starts to talk about what happened, after listening the whole story Latif recalls all the baby-sitting time he spent with Sana, and reminds about all the naughty activities she did. He is now twenty-seven and he feels that he is too young to consoles her boss, but he had no option than doing that so he consoles him and asks to take a wise decision in that matter and not to get triggered by the superstitious stuffs he says.

Waqar feels lost everything and he has been nudged by a stranger who is sitting right behind him. He tells Waqar "Salaam Bhai, why don't you try a black magic instead". Waqar, Latif and that stranger looks at each other.

Waqar and Latif realises that the stranger guy has been listening to every word they both talked and Latif initially asks him to leave the place but Waqar shows some attention towards him. Then the stranger introduces himself as an auto driver and has auto with himself he asks Waqar to come with him and he wanted to talk about the black magic "technicians" he knows, he wants Waqar to hire them and solve the problems. Even though they are Muslims, he wanted them to hire these Hindu black magic specialists as they believe demons have no specific religions.

Stranger guy takes the auto and wants Waqar to come in, Waqar who has an immense belief in these supernatural stuffs irrespective of religious beliefs gets into the auto and asks Latif to get home the bike. Latif seems half hearted with the approach of Waqar but he cannot stop his boss.

Stranger starts the auto and followed by Latif. Stranger tells Waqar that "Bhai don't be embraced as you get into this Hindu territory, in this world only gods have religions not these evil devils." Waqar smiles with pain and says "Only people have religions."

Latif stops the bike and calls Sana's mobile number which was switched off.

Latif who was shocked by this act of Sana but still he wants to help her and get her out of this thing, Latif always believed Sana would go places with her knowledge so he wants her to get rid of these.

He remembered the game Latif and Sana used to play while Sana leaves for school, which Latif says "Latif will be alright here; Will Sana be a perfect girl? Latif will be so good boy; Will Sana be a very good girl? Sana replies by blinking her eyes denoting that she accepts and obeys what all Latif says. Latif broke down remembering those good old days with little Sana.

He also panicked that Khadija would make mess of everything if she finds out Latif is helping Sana.

He reached Sana's house and asked Khadija about the problem; Latif sees Aisha also quarrelling and yelling about Sana.

Sana saw Latif hopelessly through the window. Latif told Khadija about what Waqar is about to do, Aisha responded quickly and said "Somehow her possession would end."

Khadija said "We wish to get her married to someone inside the town, we had enough of sufferings from her education stint."

Latif who wants Sana to become a graduate shocked by this statement from Khadija. He always believed and taken care of her educational support since her childhood days. Latif wants Sana to escape from the cultural and religious thing that stands as a barrier for a woman's career. Latif almost lost his final hope on Sana.

Suddenly vomiting sound ended their conversation and Sana seen vomiting behind the wall.

Meanwhile, Stranger took Waqar to a place which is filled by Hindu devotees and he got a token for consultation and gave to Waqar.

Both started to wait in the corridor until their turn comes

CHAPTER SEVEN

Chennai at night is more poetic and aesthetic than most of the aesthetic venues, those breezy night skies and heavily jammed roads horn honking everywhere but you can find each and every soul is flying like a bee to get back to home as soon as possible.

In such night Gautam decided to go to CMBT at Koyembedu which is quite far from OMR where he stayed, he packed his entire cloths and belongings with him in a huge travel bag, he was about to quit smoking for this day, yeah, he used to quit every single day. Gautam has that knack of grabbing snack in regular period of time so he bought some biscuits and Madras mixture to eat with him.

He bought a note with him, also a ball point pen in blue. He wore a shorts and t shirt and all looks set for an enchanting travel experience but he feels he is not in mood to get back to Chennai, the place he loved much more than anything but he eventually started hating it right from their parents' separation as the other two gigantic cities of South India pulled the aside. Gautam reached CMBT through bus and heads on to Pondicherry bus slot.

There he finds three buses to Pondicherry he asks one bus conductor about the timing as he needs to have dinner since he is not a guy who skip meals.

As the time goes past eight in the evening the moon has taken full charge, he boarded the less occupied bus grabbed a twenty rupees water bottle with him. Bus started to move; bus conductor begin his job to collect tickets from passengers. There are hardly four or five seats occupied in the bus.

He approximately took the centre seat, he finds a couple two rows behind him, and he guess that they might be newly married just with the amount of jewellery the woman wore and the equally weighted smile in that man's face, they were actually romancing.

Gautam pretends that he did not see that and smiles internally and he receives the SMS from "rent a resort" states that his beach resort is ready to check in.

While the bus reached the exit of the bus stand, a guy with a lungi and dirty shirt boarded the bus and sat behind those couples. He cannot take away his eyes from those couple's romance still he resisted his eyes from them. Gautam sees that man and realises that he is drunk with his face and eyes.

Suddenly that lady from the couple says something to her husband and he reacted immediately towards that drunken man. He had no clue about him shouting. Husband guy asks the conductor to disembark that drunkard man from the bus. Conductor went to him and asks him to get down but the drunkard man has money to buy tickets and he says, "You don't have any right to disembark a passenger when they paid for the tickets."

Gautam immediately asked him to come beside him and asks conductor not to throw him out. The drunkard man approaches Gautam and sits next to him and smiles with a "High" face.

Both shakes' hands and Gautam asks his name, he replied "Lurdhu".

Gautam with a bit of confusion asks again "Is that Lurdhu?".

"Yeah Lurdhu" he says.

Gautam replies "I'm Gautam" and, he added "Lord and Gautam haha Lord.Gautam"

Lurdhu asks Gautam "Sir, you're also drunk?"

Gautam laughs and says "No, I don't need to drunk now because my life is as high as anything so don't want to add extra substance to make it higher".

Lurdhu says "Sir, I can't get your life matter"

"Even I do" says Gautam.

Bus now started to sail fluently on the sea of traffic jam that greater Chennai City has constructed itself.

CHAPTER EIGHT

A tour down the memory lane started between the sweet pan caked couples Mr. Paul and Mrs. Madeline, they were solemnly sure that they are going to love for some time.

"That was a pretty normal day in Pondicherry," said Paul.

"No, wait! That is not normal day for me it was strange so do not dramatize so much" Madeline says in hurry.

"Where's your sick tone went now?" Paul asked

Now Madeline looks at Paul with a pretty confused face and said "What are you expecting me to do? To hug and cuddle like the ones who love these days? I am not the one among those I romanticise love feel"

Paul stood up and saw the strong commanding face of Madeline and said "This is what I saw way back on that pretty normal day back in Pondicherry"

In December 1971, when young Paul and James were on a tour to Pondicherry to participate in an art competition held at French Colony. Both were so young in their mid-twenties both wore striped shirts. Paul took his paintings made from vegetable colours that gave him a good reception from his hometown back in Glenmorgan, that painting was inspired from a bible incident. Jesus was crucified to death, he was carrying the cross on his shoulder and forced to walk, his mother Mary saw his sufferings and cried. Paul took that as an inspiration and drew a painting by changing the biblical fact as Mary kisses Jesus on forehead that heals the entire wound, he had.

This was placed for a show and many felt so soothing and emotional and even some Christians felt bible scenarios should not have changed but still Paul's intention of showing mother's love can heal anything is being received so lovely.

Paul stands near to an old French warrior statue but he cannot pronounce or read the name written on the statue. He has given many attempts to read as of now.

Many came to praise Paul and gifted some money for him, which he told James, that would be helpful for the development of Sir Alister Wood street. Then also a school principal whose entire school came for an educational tour to this competition met him and praised about the painting for some time.

Meanwhile James was roaming around the streets and waiting outside the art gallery where the competition was held. He saw a French school's teacher who seemed a young lady with an English essence explaining about Paul's painting to her colleagues and James rushed to Paul and talked about how people outside love his painting.

Principal wants his school's drawing teacher to meet Paul and asked his assistant to call her. Assistant calls Ms. Madeline Evy who is a young teacher from French colony wearing a hard black spectacle with a gown and shortened hair and looks a typical half Indian and half French, came and she has been introduced to Paul by Principal as a drawing teacher of the school. James now nudges Paul and mentioned that this young lady was the one who was praising your painting outside. Principal leaves the place and asks Madeline to speak some words with Paul. James also makes his way outside to have a cup of tea. Now both

Paul and Madeline left alone there near the painting. Both stood short of words and Madeline started the conversation by saying "I guess the painting spoke more words than you". Paul smiled back and said "thank you my pleasure and glad you liked it". Madeline nodded his head and asked a question, "Mr. Paul If you don't mind, can you please explain what made you do this?"

"Love" said Paul.

Both were standing under a statue of a French Warrior, whose name is very tough for Paul to pronounce.

Paul tries to hide the fact that he cannot read the name of that warrior, so he stops trying.

Madeline gave a short smile and said "That is too rough. I needed more fair answer but yeah as an artist you do not reveal your secrets and sources, right?"

Paul cannot explain how he struggles to speak with a woman of his age and searches for his friend James who almost absconded from the place.

Paul then replied "Actually it is love, not the sins we make. Love is what everyone needs, it is priceless"

Madeline again smiled and asked "Love of a mother, that's so natural and easy to sketch for boys who are always close to their mothers"

Paul replied "But I don't have such one I believe my place is my mother, The valley of Glenmorgan, Sir Alister Wood street."

Madeline shocked and apologized Paul for making him feel emotional about mother and she intentionally wanted to change topic so she asked about this place. Paul explained how beautiful his place was he told about his entire place has filled with clouds and snows and about his work of getting the things from above town to Glenmorgan valley.

Madeline started to admire him and Paul looks so thirsty and sweating to speak with Madeline. She then decided to leave but she wants to talk more but the anxiety level of Paul troubled the conversation.

Madeline said "Bye" half-heartedly and Paul stops her.

"Shall we meet at the shore in the evening?" said Paul

Madeline stood silent and twisted her hand band and hesitantly said "I have to think about it"'

Paul almost lost his confidence and feels too embraced to see her.

Madeline the replied "Yeah, I have to think so give me some time I'll definitely tell you when we meet at six this evening?" She smiled and walked back to join her colleagues and moved from the place.

James who just finished his snacks cravings outside came back and nudged Paul, "Did you really asked her?"

"I think so," said Paul.

French colony is one of the beautiful places at Pondicherry, both Paul and James roamed the entirc French colony until noon and both failed to see Madeline again. Finally, they came back to their room. Paul was watching the clock passes every second to reach six in the evening. In the meantime, he went to bazar to buy a beautiful ear ring for her which is the first gift he buys for Madeline too. He bought the necklace and he also wants to alter a bit short as he predicted a close neck dollar would enhance her beauty much more.

Clock reached six in the evening, beautiful Pondicherry beach was waiting to witness something eternal in few moments, Paul came in first and found a small hut and started waiting for Madeline who gave a hint. Time passed by still he has not found any traces of Madeline reaching the shore, kids were playing on the shore happily and he got disappointed and turned back to go home, there he saw a shadow under a street light having a flower, he looked up to see the entire universal laws of power and light sources enhanced the face of Madeline.

Paul welcomed her and greeted with a smile, Madeline spoke nothing but hazed the sea shore and the kids playing happily on the sand.

They took the sand path to shore, Madeline asked "Would you like to have a coffee with me?" "My pleasure," said Paul.

There were so many heritage coffee bars seen at Pondicherry but Paul is so scared as he could not afford such coffees at those bars. He checked his purse and that was noted by Madeline. She took him for a coffee and Paul feels little embraced.

But still Paul wanted to show something more romantic than coffee so he chose the Moon. He took him to the nearest fishing harbour and jumped into the anchored boat and asks Madeline to close her eyes. Excited Madeline, closed her eyes with curiosity and she was asked to sit inside the boat turned towards the sea.

Paul whispered near her ears, and placed the ear rings on her palm he bought for her and said "Sometimes people with less acquittance turns out to be the best tuner of our radar, here's to the moon and sea, Ms. Madeline wants to see".

Paul asked Madeline to open her eyes and what Madeline saw was something dreamier than reality, The close cuddle of Moon and the sea.

Madeline stopped Paul from traveling down the memory lane of both and back to 2013," Hello that was so romantic still I have seen those scenes even before you took me". Old Paul replies to old Madeline with seeing her face with all the love in the world, "But I know for the first time you loved the scene, I know at that moment Madeline wants to see the Moon and sea together for rest of life with Paul". He also noticed the necklace on Madeline's neck that was hanging around for almost more than forty years in front of the eyes of Paul.

Madeline's sick voice troubled her from speaking with the same tone but somehow managed her husband to lend a pan cake for her. She feels very cold and the blanket she has did not have a proper stitching at one place which allows the cold to come in haunt her. Paul went to take the pan cake for her, he came back and sat at bed and Madeline pulled himself out of blanket and rest her head in Paul's lap. Paul nudged her twice and asked her to wake up and have pan cake, she asked him to feed her.

"Paul, do you have anything to say?" asked Madeline.

"No" replied Paul with loud voice.

Madeline asked Paul a favour, "I thought we would go to France one day, but we lived our entire life here at Glenmorgan, I have a wish! I wish someday we go to France and express our love with no inner feelings that we are not born to love we are born to love, and also, I want to see what's left in my family which I left for the love in you"

Paul felt shocked yet excited as he has not heard such words from his wife in all these years, Madeline said "I wish we had children; I wish they have children too after all we are oldies, right? Mr. Paul."

"We are, yeah, we are but I feel not old yet to tell these in past at least we can try our best in rest of our life to find the maximum of what you told..." said Paul and he stopped his talk a bit and noticed something strange in Madeline who was resting in his lap, Paul looked up and then looked down to see Madeline resting without breath in his lap, the he ended his sentence ".... Ms. Madeline".

Paul has no clue what to do, he stunned and started hazing the paintings around his house, Madeline's voice filled his ears and he also checked her beat stopped and the pure silence slowly filled that house.

Loud shouts, commands, arguments, scolding, more and more love phrases have ended, the commanding yet loving voice of Madeline has stopped.

Paul still can't believe his wife is dead, he took her and placed on her bed and remembered her last words to feed her the cake so he took the pancake and placed inside her mouth and started calling her name, and also he starts to tell her a new story about what he saw above the mountains, he asked "Madeline, if you are not responding I am not bringing carrots anymore specially for you..." by saying this Paul got his teared fed up in his eye and throat stopped and he started to cry and he cried loudly. Entire Alister Wood street of Glenmorgan left stunned by the loud shout of Paul.

Now Henry and Mary heard Paul crying loudly and they both rushed to his house, they both stood stunned seeing the activities of Paul.

Paul seemed rotating the house and seeing the paintings of Madeline one by one. Mary got scared and ran back to her house. Henry came in consoled Paul to stop crying. Paul told him about what happened and Henry also felt like Madeline is still in the house courtesy of painted walls.

Paul wants Madeline to rest behind her house so he wants to do the entire rituals within his house.

As the dawn comes by Henry called the church's father to do the funeral rituals for Madeline and asked Mary to stay inside house as they have a kid with them.

Church's father Louis came in a cycle and he found Henry digging the hole and, he bought the coffin for Madeline. Paul started crying again and he filled those coffins with some carrots, pan cakes and some drawings which Madeline drew at her college and Pondicherry times. Henry feels emotional as his father James talked about Madeline and Paul's love story a lot.

Paul also took the ear rings from Madeline which he bought for her few moments before her death which almost resembled the one which he gifted way back in 1971 at French colony.

Tears fed up on Henry's face, Father Louis noticed him and consoled Henry, and Paul was left near Madeline's coffin.

Several bible verses were read and rituals are done by Father alongside Paul.

Only three attended the funeral, they buried Madeline right behind Paul's house.

Paul went back to his home alone without Madeline but with her memories, all happened within one night Henry stayed along with Paul for some days but still Paul is listening to the commands of his love of life, Madeline.

Few days later Paul started to paint another painting of his wife Madeline but he couldn't complete it properly as his mind is not stable and fresh as before as he used to be with Madeline's presence.

He even failed to get milk and groceries for the people of Alister Wood Street, and Henry took charge for that job for few days but eventually he could not capitalise the work as Paul did not allow anybody from that street to work hard.

Exactly fifteen days later, one day when Henry was bringing the milk and groceries for his shop and the people of Alister Wood street, he accidently went across an unknown path and left stranded, the dark clouds and the chillness gave the chills to his spines.

But he was rescued by an old man whom seems to be the same age as of Paul, dressed up like an army personnel wore a blue shirt with dark blue pant and holds a chain with whistle in his neck, he promised to direct him towards down to the Alister Wood street inside the Valley. The old man introduced himself as the security guard for reservoir dam of Glenmorgan very close to this valley.

“Hey Henry, I know you as a kid! I am sure Paul is not okay, what happened to him,” said that old man.

Henry understood that he claims to be the friend of Paul and replied “He lost his love.”

CHAPTER NINE

That place is so strange for Waqar but he convinced himself that he has no other option than black magic to get rid of her daughter's possession. In their turn they got in and the stranger guy whose name is still not known by Waqar until that Hindu Godman called him "Kumar" Kumar told the entire family issue of Waqar and that Godman asks Kumar to stay outside. Waqar sat with no clues as he is unaware of all these Hindu practices so listens to that Godman so calmly and keenly. Godman asks Waqar to get her daughter tomorrow night for a special ritual and added he should not tell this to anybody as that was also a part of this ritual. Godman also said that Kumar will take of buying all things which are necessary for the rituals.

Kumar who is waiting outside is ready with the list of products which was given by one of the lady assistants of that Godman. Both Waqar and Kumar looked at each other moved from that place.

At home, Khadija is cleaning the vomit of Sana, and Latif is just looking at Sana helping her, after Khadija leaves that place to assist Aisha, Latif approached Sana to ask about what happened. Sana initially refused to look at the face of Latif but later saw and started leaking tears.

Latif questioned Sana "Are you okay with the abortion?"

Sana shocked by the words of Latif. He asked again and looked into the eyes of Sana who looked confused, He also added "I don't want to know anything about whom and when, I just need you to grab a college degree as per as your wish, nothing should be a barrier for your career, I repeat nothing!"

Sana looked tensed and she has broken down once again.

Latif also warned about the local Godman coming to her and he also wants to save her from getting abused as he known about them earlier, but the ardent belief of Waqar and his anxiety stopped him from saying.

Latif took the responsibility for safeguarding Sana also saving her from getting married, he saw Sana and warned her to stay calm and said "I'll do the rest you just stay focused". Sana stood with the confused face. Latif goes out of the house and dialled to his friend Sriram's number who is in Chennai.

"Sriram, can you do me a favour?" Latif spoke through the call to Sriram.

He came back to Sana and asked her about the date of Engineering Entrance exam which Sana applied back in December 2012, Sana is not aware of the details so Latif found out the date and it is day after next day April 18th. Latif slaps his head and saw Sana's face turning red and another wave of tears started to rise. Latif immediately consoled her and told her not to worry.

"Get your books and dresses, pack everything you need, take the pills, just elope," said Latif. Sana looks confused because a guy who is more like a brother figure to her, taught her everything morally, now saying this, but clearly, they have no option than this to give entrance exam for Engineering which is day after next day. He also gave Sriram's number written on a slip and told her "Now its 1.30 PM, you must be ready to catch the 8.45 PM train from

Rameswaram to Chennai and he clutched the slip in the hands of Sana and ordered her to escape from the threat that is upcoming to her in her house and he left the place.

Sana has no time think about "plan B" as she has only one way to live her life, she immediately took the books she read got three dresses and the pills she was prescribed at the hospital earlier and packed the things. Khadija entered the room suddenly and Sana stunned in shock slowly Khadija came nearer to her, Sana almost lost her nerve and started sweating, Khadija then gave that rose petals filled water to drink and leaves the room. Sana now pulled out the travel bag she packed from under the cot.'

Waqar and Kumar bought the things for the rituals at the nearer shop and Kumar consoled Waqar not to worry and everything will be okay.

Kumar then takes a leave from that place and asked Waqar to get her daughter sharply at 9 PM to the Godman's place. Waqar agreed and proceeded back to home.

Kumar took his auto to the Godman's place and entered inside the secret room and started waiting, the Godman came in for lunch break.

"Where is my commission?" Kumar asked.

Godman gave a reaction which tells Kumar is always fond of commission than work. "Will be given to you once the project is done," said the Godman.

Latif was drinking tea and talking to Sriram through phone call who is an electronic service dealer who sell spare parts and does mobile service at reasonably low cost. He resides at T. Nagar and works in a shop at Saidapet. Latif told him about the entire issue Sana is facing and he wants Sana to write that exam first also wants her to abort that child as that shouldn't be a barrier for her education. Sriram agreed to help and he also promised that he would guide her. Latif receives a call immediately after he cuts the call with Sriram, Waqar called. He informed about the rituals and explained about the procedures that Godman told. Latif got shocked and confirms what he sensed was completely right as the scenarios are as same in the last case too, Latif asked Waqar to stop this and Waqar replied in anger through phone "Latif, please do not interfere! Just do what I said"

Latif said nothing and cuts the call, Waqar got back home and Sana listened to chappal sound of her father and hide the bag and the books she was studying, Waqar opened the door and said about the rituals.

"Get ready and pray to the god" said Waqar.

Sana sat at the floor resting her head on the bed, and thinks about the little womb is swimming inside her uterus, but she also feels worried about that little womb is about to die in few days' times.

Godman's place is getting ready for the rituals and the lady assistants of the Godman entered the ritual room and decorated the place, Kumar finally came in and acknowledged the work but Godman immediately asked him to stay out of the entire process. Kumar hesitantly leaves the place, the time is ticking to the evening, everyone stayed tensed Waqar, Latif, Kumar and more importantly Sana whom seemed to be super tensed about what to happen as she has taken the decision of her life.

CHAPTER TEN

Lurdhu and Gautam are chatting as the bus reached East Coast Road (ECR) from Chennai city. ECR always gives a vibe that has both sides, in fact it has so many faces. A long stretch towards south of Chennai, the land of Pallavas enlighten you with excitement! Amusement parks around the corner of Bay of Bengal will leave you amused by its larger-than-life experience. But both Lurdhu and Gautam are involved in discussing right from national politics to local body politics first up.

"It will come to an end!" said Gautam.

Lurdhu on the other hand says "But I'm not sure people will change the party that ruled for ten long years."

"Nothing is in our hands, it's all about the fate of country" said Gautam with a gasping voice.

"Fate is in our hands next year" Lurdhu replied with some determination in his face.

Lurdhu seems so desperate to know about Gautam but Gautam didn't open up much as he didn't want to tell the sad things to anyone. He also decided to hide his past relationship to anyone new he meets.

But Gautam wants to know about Lurdhu a common bus stand drunkard guy whose hub would be most probably the bus stand here in Tamil Nadu.

Gautam started calling Lurdhu as "Anna" which means a brother in Tamil.

He started with asking Lurdhu about his alcoholic beverage's brand and rate, now Lurdhu started explaining who he is and what has actually happened.

Lurdhu is a native of Chennai who works as a share auto driver, he has 2 sons elder one studying ninth grade and the younger one is sixth grade in a school at Choolaimedu. Lurdhu explained about his little family to Gautam.

“Anna, what about your wife?” asked Gautam.

Lurdhu shakes head horizontally and Gautam realised that his wife is no more and apologised for asking.

“So, the boys must be alone at home, right? Why would you be travelling at this night” Gautam asked with a soft voice that Lurdhu has not listened to for quite few days.

Lurdhu has not had greatest of past few days or so, three months ago he gave a sum of forty-five thousand rupees to a man named Sundaram who is the neighbour of Lurdhu in Choolaimedu who works in an ice factory at Chennai harbour. Sundaram borrowed the money and promised to return within fifteen days' time. Sundaram has two wives on live in Choolaimedu and the other one lives in Amjinkarai which is pretty much close to Choolaimedu.

Sundaram's first wife, named Rani. The couple has a daughter named Akhila, aged twelve, Rani stayed unsatisfied with his husband Sundaram as he found another partner despite, she being alive. Second wife of Sundaram, named Shanthi who is fifteen years younger than Sundaram.

Lurdhu always helped Sundaram in many of his activities except the fact of marrying a girl who is fifteen years younger to him, Lurdhu also warned that he would lose his wife Rani because of this but Sundaram did not worried about anything what Lurdhu said and married Shanthi, whose native is almost unknown but some people says that she is from Nellore, Andra Pradesh.

One day Lurdhu was driving share auto around Nungambakkam, Sundaram rushed to Lurdhu through bike and asked money urgently by telling his daughter Akhila has hit her puberty and he needs to spend money for the mandatory ritual function.

Lurdhu sooner accepts with no hesitation as he has seen Akhila grown up right from her younger days. Very next day, Lurdhu withdraws the money from the post office bank which he deposited for his children. Sundaram promised that he would return as soon as his loan sanctioned in his office at harbour.

Lurdhu completely believed his friend so he lends his money.

"I lend my entire savings of forty-five thousand rupees to him" said Lurdhu.

Suddenly phone rings for Gautam in the bus, a call from "Rent a resort" Pondicherry. Gautam attends it.

"Hi, this is Sushmita from "Rent a resort" Pondicherry! Since you booked a resort, we will provide you a cottage which has only one bed, kitchen, and a place to chill with the sea view" said the voice over the phone.

Gautam replied "No, I need two beds, we are two! Yeah".

"Okay sir, kindly tell the name of your guest" asked the voice over the phone.

"Lurdhu" said Gautam.

Lurdhu turns at him and gave a clueless reaction.

Gautam said "Yeah, you are staying with me Anna"

Lurdhu hesitantly shakes head with a blinking eye swiftly, suddenly bus stops and the conductor shouts and wakes up everyone for the "Rest stop"

Almost everyone in the bus gets down for the rest stop, an old Tamil song "Innisai paadi varum" plays loudly which helps to wake up everyone in the buses even they fell asleep.

Gautam and Lurdhu goes to the shop, Gautam asked for a cigarette and offered Lurdhu a one which he denied. Sound of waves along with the horns of buses that passing by.

Lurdhu opens his purse and saw his family photo and feels missing his sons.

Gautam came to know that place is "Odiyur", from a tea seller.

Suddenly a gang of three men came to Gautam and one of those guys asked him "Brother, have you seen a skinny girl wearing half hijab?" Another one added "She will be aging around eighteen or nineteen". Gautam cannot listen to them due to heavy sound of the song that plays in the shop, but he managed to answer them by asking them to repeat the query and ask quite louder.

Then, Gautam replied "No"

Immediately the gang revolved that entire rest stop's café and bathroom keeper and rushed onto their car, one of that gang still hanging around outside with full frustration.

He came to Lurdhu and consoled said "Just few hours from here, we can make it very soon". He also added "Okay na, what happened further?"

Meanwhile, Gautam accidentally sees his bag shakes in his bus seat through the window he senses something wrong and he feels someone is stealing something from his bag so he immediately rushed into his bus seat and he saw a skinny girl with half hijab trying to hide herself beneath the big tall traveling bag of Gautam.

"Hey" said Gautam.

The girl turned towards Gautam.

That girl kept her hands together and pleaded not to tell anyone and she cried.

Gautam sees that gang hanging around and searching for this girl while he also recognises that girl is wounded, he immediately realises that she is being molested by that gang, meantime Lurdhu rushes into the bus following Gautam and he also understood the situation.

Now, that gang takes the car and leaves and Gautam notices that the car heads towards Chennai.

Bus driver and the bus passengers gets in the bus and finally conductors start checking the head count of the passengers, which he regularly does at the rest stop.

Both Gautam and Lurdhu looked at each other, both understood that they have a plan now.

Conductor came to check the head count and Gautam kept his big tall travelling bag in his lap, Lurdhu starts blinking heavily and conductor already has had a heated argument with both so he went silently.

Bus moves, now Gautam moves the bag and kept aside and that girl came out from between his legs by thanking him.

"Who are you?" asked Gautam.

"Sana" replied Sana.

CHAPTER ELEVEN

Henry and that old man walked through that dense forest; old man guided through a narrow path which is often used by Paul on his times during work."

"Here's the gift that Paul gave me in all these years of our friendship, he must be very sad now," said the old man. He mentioned that narrow path.

Henry also thinks about the situation of Paul and said "He never missed a single of his valley trip in all these years but this situation demanded such a hard one, I miss him, I feel he just recovers soo..."

Old man stopped him saying that word "recover soon" and said "Who needs to recover? A man who has the soul of an entire livelihood or a man who served for a village in his entire lifetime? I must see him soon, come on"

Henry turned towards that reservoir dam and asks about that to the old man.

"I have partners, kid!" said old man.

Henry is so tired and much afraid of the wild animal scares, his faces show everything to that old man who is keenly watching Henry, he also panics about the situation of his child down at the Alister Wood Street who is waiting for the milk.

Old man then started talking briefly to Henry, "When both James and Paul were in your age, they both use to carry one another on their shoulder to walk past this valley, but you haven't seemed to be much stronger as them, isn't you kid?"

Henry nods his head with tired and gasps.

Old man again started to mock Henry by saying, "My boy Henry, Elephants seen alone are more dangerous, they feel insecure and starts attacking us!"

"Why would you say that now? I am so scared to be here" Henry pleaded towards that old man with a shaky voice.

Old man laughed for few seconds and stopped suddenly, he turned his head in sideways and checked for something, Henry holding the milk can and the vegetables looks even more scary.

Then, old man asked him to keep quiet, suddenly an Elephant with heavy tusk produces its trumpeting sound.

Entire scene made Henry scare as he was stuck in a hell.

Old man stood like a statue and asked Henry to follow the same. Henry controlling his tears and stood like a statue.

Elephant comes closer to both and sniffs heavily, this makes Henry to go crazy and he starts shouting. Now, Elephant rises its trunk and starts trumpeting again heavily.

Suddenly a clapping sound comes from that narrow path to Alister Wood street, and the elephant turns around towards the sound, there stands Paul with bundle packs of chili powder in his hand.

Paul snaps the packets of chili powder and elephant got distracted and starts to run away, soon Paul throws the other packet from his back bag to the old man and he started to snap the packet right in front of elephant's eyes. Henry who is almost fainted watching all these stunts by the two old men.

Elephant ran away to its path.

Now both Paul and the old man gasps and relaxes,

"Jacob, it's been a time," said Paul.

"Missed you man" said Jacob the old man.

"But you never missed your valley trip, Uncle Paul"

All three men Paul, Jacob, Henry started their way to Alister Wood street.

They reached the street almost at nine in the evening, Henry got home immediately as his wife is waiting for the milk with her child.

Paul guided Jacob to his place to show the tombstone of Madeline Evy, and Jacob saw that with a tear-filled eye. Henry chopping carrot and lady's finger to make a masala to stuff inside bread roll he made, and, he left some bread rolls uncooked which he said was made my Madeline just before his death.

Henry knocks the door; he came with his child and his wife Mary. Paul immediately starred at Henry.

Henry shouts at Paul as he ordered not to cook, Mary gave the food which was made in their home, suddenly a neighbour call her name at James tea stall; Mary rushes back to stall with her kid.

Henry and Jacob look at each other and Jacob turns his eyes towards the beautiful paintings of Madeline that Paul painted.

Paul having the ear rings that he bought finally for Madeline and sat silently.

Jacob breaks the silence, and asks "So what's next Paul? See you being here and doing nothing does not going to bring your wife back, you must move on, everyone needs to see your smile and work back! I literally cannot see you like this; the entire reservoir dam water sound asks about you to me."

Slowly rain started to pour outside, Henry went out and had a glance about his shop, he came back to see Paul crying by resting on a painting of Madeline.

Paul said "She wanted to visit France, that was the last wish she told me, I am a coward I'm a loser".

Jacob denied and consoled Paul. Henry looks furious and started yelling at Paul.

"I got it now; he needs to go to France? I can sense his scam, yes you are a coward, Uncle Paul," said Henry.

"Just like your father, you care for me just like your father, but not everyone can be your father, if my James is alive, He would've booked the tickets for me and asked me to pack my bags, yeah it is my fault to be alive without my mates, first your father, then your mother and now my Madeline, I'm too old now for the earth Mr. James Jr" Paul said with soften shaky voice.

Henry looked Paul furiously.

"You know, I bought this for her, I feels her soul must be sailing on the streets of Pondicherry, I need to go, I need to find out is there anyone left for Madeline there, I would find any small hole to find Madeline's family, James calling, Madeline calling, Holy mother Mary and her son Jesus calling" said Paul and he opens the old painting of him which he drew and kept at Pondicherry forty years ago in 1971.

Henry still starring at him and started shouting, "Uncle Paul, enough is enough do you think?"

Jacob stopped Henry and asked Paul "You are going to Pondicherry with the ear ring you bought for your Madeline"

Henry now looking cluelessly, Jacob confirms again "Yes Paul, you are going to Pondicherry I'll arrange the rest, until then it's Henry, the owner of James tea stall with take care of milk man job Alister Wood street"

Henry shakes head by denying and Jacob throws the back bag of Paul to Henry and said "You are ready to go"

Next day Paul is blessed by father Louis and the ear ring is also blessed with holy water, and Louis was paid some money by Jacob and Henry who completely hates all these activities pouring tea in his shop nearby Paul's house. Paul carries a small travel bag which contains a painting brush, few dresses, those ear rings, and a special letter he wrote for Madeline last night.

Jacob and Paul hire a horse taxi, which is the only way to go out of the town and then they board the jeep and heads to Glenmorgan main village, it is only the third time that Paul is leaving Glenmorgan, first time when James's wife Ruby was pregnant to give birth for Henry, next for that competition where he saw Madeline and now for the same Madeline just to heal the memories and the wound his heart has conceived.

They reached Mettupalayam on a bus and connected to Coimbatore.

Jacob said that Paul should board "MAQ Chennai express, that would go Chennai via Trichy, as there are no direct trains for Pondicherry from Coimbatore or any other residing places, Paul should change train from Trichy junction and go to Pondicherry via Thanjavur – Kumbakonam – Chidambaram.

Jacob also said "Paul, this train will be reaching Trichy at exactly 9.55 PM, and the next train you should board arrives at 10.40 PM so you should wait at the junction and find the platform for the next train and board carefully"

Paul received everything and nods his head.

"Another thing, the second train is also not going to Pondicherry! You should get down at Chidambaram at and change to bus to Pondicherry, the busses are so frequent there, remember! To Trichy then wait until 10.40 PM next to Chidambaram at 1.30 AM and to bus stand board the bus to Pondicherry; kindly find out, in some busses it will be written as Pudhucherry." Said Jacob.

This seems to be Himalayan task for Paul as he never visited those places before, but the courage of Paul upheld before any of his hesitations.

MAQ Chennai express departure time from Coimbatore Junction is 3.45 PM (i.e) 15.45 PM, time is now 1.45 PM.

Jacob bought the lunch and the body of Paul does not obey the heat temperature here at Coimbatore, so he was sweating heavily and wiping his cloth every two minutes.

Jacob feels pity about Paul, but he has no option to cure Paul from his mental trauma.

Jacob takes out a cell phone from his pocket and asks Paul to keep.

"No, I don't know how to use it" Paul denies.

But Jacob forced him to have and starts teaching how to use that old model colour phone. "If you receive a call you have to press the green button, and if you want to call me, press number one and I'll be speaking from the other end".

Paul still hesitates to have that mobile phone, but obeys Jacob finally and accepts it.

Train arrived, both Paul and Jacob finishes lunch and Jacob gets inside the train in an unreserved compartment, which was mostly occupied but Jacob somehow found a place for Paul and kept his bag. Paul's face filled with fear and excitement like a kid, Train horns and it is about to depart.

Jacob gets down, Paul says "bye" to Jacob and now he repeats the exact instructions what he was saying for an entire hour before the train arrived.

"Paul, this train will be reaching Trichy at exactly 9.55 PM, and the next train you should board arrives at 10.40 PM so you should wait at the junction and find the platform for the next train and board carefully, another thing, the second train is also not going to Pondicherry! You should get down at Chidambaram at and change to bus to Pondicherry, the busses are so frequent there, remember! To Trichy then wait until 10.40 PM next to Chidambaram at 1.30 AM and to bus stand board the bus to Pondicherry kindly finds out, in some busses it will be written as Pudhucherry" Jacob repeated from the platform by seeing Paul through the window as the train stars moving.

After listening to everything, Paul calmy replied, "Take care of Alister Wood street and the kiddo Henry, Tata cheerio"

CHAPTER TWELVE

It was very normal after noon in Rameswaram for most of the people, other than Sana who decides to elope. Latif was seen waiting at the railway station with the bag that Sana packed. Kumar is rushing in his auto to Mandapam which is next to pamban bridge where the closest wine shop is located as Rameswaram does not have wine shops inside the town. Godman is all set for another ritual in his place, one of his assistants calls Waqar but he did not pick up. Waqar is bathing in his home to get ready, he also asked his wife Khadija and his mother to keep this thing secret as the other fellow Muslims. So, the rituals that the Godman is going to conduct is kept very secret, but the faces of Khadija and Aisha clearly indicates that they are hiding something.

Waqar who is now ready to go asks Sana to get ready, Immediately Sana came out of the room with well-dressed and seems like she got ready already. Minutes ago, he gave the bag and the books to read to Latif, who is now waiting at the railway station with the tickets. Aisha closes her eyes as she did not want to see djinn possessed Sana. Khadija wears a rope on Sana's hand and asks her to stay calm and with zipped mouth.

Waqar checks his mobile to see that the Godman tried to call him twice, he called back to intimate that they are on the way.

Loud sound of "Allah-hu-Akbar" plays in nearby mosque, indicating the noon prayer time.

Scooter starts, Sana sees Aisha and asks for a minute, she ran back to her bedroom and had a glance at everything and, she cries at her things and also at the first hijab she wore. She took her mobile, opened his boyfriend's messages which she did not received a proper reply, she sends a "hi" to him again, waited for two seconds to get that SMS delivered.

It got delivered.

Then, she sends "Thank you coward, for giving me courage! You could have asked me straight away the thing you wanted, at least I would have still had the faith in the word "love" enjoy".

Sana leaves the room, and she gave a look at Khadija and stops for a second, but the scooter horn of her father urges her to "get out" Sana gets on the scooter.

Waqar moves the scooter, Sana sees her house with plenty of memories, they crossed their street and Sana gave a glance at every place she grown up playing and watches mosque where she used to visit along with her father when she was kid, then they crossed the school which Sana studied and now she saw the ice cream van where Sana and her ex-boyfriend spent more time after school, then she found the nearby tea shop where he had seen his ex-boyfriend more often.

Slowly scooter stops near a building which replicates an old horror-haunted house, Sana gets down from the scooter and sees the building with fear, Waqar immediately pushed him inside the building, and it gave strange feelings for a girl who never known about any other religion than Islam.

Both Waqar and Sana were greeted initially by the workers of that place, and the assistants of the Godman were seen making up the place for the rituals.

Sana pleaded “No, please I’m so scared”

Waqar got angry and said “You are not scared of other things, right? Let the possession runs off from you”

“No, please I beg you I’m so scared of these things please leave me alone I’ll run far away from you, please I beg you” said Sana and cried loudly suddenly the assistants held the hands of Sana and she started shaking off from them.

Waqar seeing all these gymnastics by Sana, came forward and slapped her heavily. Instantly Sana fainted and the assistants took her into the Godman’s room. Godman came out and asked him not to disturb until he calls him back.

Waqar agreed.

Godman entered the room and the assistants closed the door immediately.

In Mandapam wine shop, fully rushed evening, Kumar is waiting for his turn to get his drink, he asked for a brandy to the shopkeeper but he has less money so the shopkeeper scold him. He came back outside and starts searching for some company to share the drink with.

He found a man who is seen standing near a tree and drinking alone, he seems to be a bit high. Kumar decides to approach him. That man is tall and looks fit enough to smash at least ten people and he wore several Hindu religious threads and has a splash of white ash, which Hindus apply for devotional beliefs. Kumar approaches him to buy a quarter amount bottle for a spare and he promises to pay him at Rameswaram.

That man denied first and asks Kumar to leave the place, but Kumar started pleading as he forgot to bring the purse with him, and he will pay back from his brother at Rameswaram.

"You know what? My brother actually rules entire Rameswaram, he is the biggest top tier Godmans of the town," said Kumar.

"Who is your brother? Lord Shiva?" asked that man.

"No, he is even bigger, has control over anything, he will provide you the money, so now lend me a quarter" Kumar pleaded again.

"Lord Shiva is the only lord of land Rameswaram, so I don't care about whomever rules there now, Ram from Ramayana worshiped Lord Shiva there, even he knows who rules there" that man replied with proud as well as trippy face.

"Boss, I can sense you are high enough with more stuffs, but I'm yet to sip a drop" Kumar asked him with one last hope.

That man finally agreed to lend him a quarter and asks him to take to Rameswaram to collect the money from his Godman brother and he also wants to meet him. Kumar instantly agreed with no hesitation as he believes that Godman will give him the commission money he owes.

Kumar drank a quarter and again repeats it, he also banged so many side dishes to accompany that drink, still he argues with the bar attender that nothing has perfect tase of salt in it,

"I need saltier," said Kumar.

He then started to speak more and raised his voice to that man, now Kumar asked the bar shopkeeper for another quarter and that man stops him and said "I need to go, it's getting late you moron".

Kumar then stood up and searched for the auto keys in his pocket, but he could not find it. But that man pokes him and shows the key in his hands indicates that he will be riding the auto.

Both started through pamban bridge.

Godman wakes up Sana in his room by splashing water on to her face. Sana again reacted vigorously by shouting and Godman asks his assistants to leave the room through the next door inside the room.

Sana slowed her voice and the Godman started talking,

"Remember girl, you have committed mistake by doing all these unwanted things with a boy, so things are not new for you! And you better not to tell your father, and you know what? He was about to kill you, I bet he was that furious when he came to meet me! But I consoled him, I will be giving you a life, you either give birth or abort that is none of my choices but current pleasure is mine, I don't torture you, I don't want to kill your baby right here, but you should heal me and I'll deal you" said the Godman and gave evil laugh.

Sana who started crying again and asks him to leave her. She even begged that she will pay money from her father but to leave her without touching.

"Sana, don't act smart, I know you like this," said the Godman.

He also insisted Sana to pull off her pants as she has committed the mistake in accordance with vagina, so he wants to do the ritual there.

Sana heavily shocked and almost tried to open the inside door that but Godman pulled her inside and removed her pant. Sana falls and completely broke. Godman then, undresses his top and came towards Sana.

Time is ticking for the train to start; Latif is waiting at the railway station.

That man drives the auto and Kumar guides him from behind.

Sana is crying and fall down half nude and the Godman approaches her and Sana starts being silent, then the Godman held her both legs and sat down.

Instantly Sana starts urinating on the Godman's face, immediately Godman lost his grip from her legs but Sana held his head uptight with her legs resting on his shoulders and continued urinating.

Meanwhile, Kumar and that man reached to the Godman's place and the man asks for money. Kumar came in and saw Waqar waiting outside immediately he took a turn and asks that man to come in another way.

Sana took off her legs from his shoulders and wore the pant and the Godman stands up and stuck freeze in shock, suddenly Kumar opens the door in high mood saw the Godman standing with a wet face, he came close to the Godman and licked his face and said "This is much saltier."

That man saw everything and understood the situation and asked Sana not to worry. He started smashing both Kumar and the Godman heavily and asked Sana, "Where do you want to go?"

Sana saw both the ways, the door which is close to her father and the door which paved way for the outside world and remembers Latif has been waiting at the railway station. Sana chooses the later and asks that man to drop him at the railway station.

That man saw both and takes the key and decides to drop Sana at the railway station and said "This is end of this mafia"

He drives the auto to the railway station and drops her gave her money which Sana refused and later accepted.

He stops Sana and blessed her with the white ash powder, and applied on her head by chanting Shiva's mantras. Sana smiles and thanked him. She entered the platform.

That man called to a number through phone and said "Hey, this is Eswaran speaking, are our boys free now?......"

Time is almost there, Rameswaram – Chennai Egmore train is about to start and finally at 17:45 from Rameswaram railway station, Sana found Latif and he ran towards her and embarked her in unreserved compartment, and told not to worry about the situation here. Latif then gave a box which contains a cell phone with new sim inserted, he also said "I'll call to this number tomorrow morning, and I'll guide you, don't worry."

Sana receives the box and keeps inside her bag.

"I will manage everything here; you take care of your things! You should eat well, I kept the money at three places in your bag and your certificates," said Latif.

Sana stands at the footboard and says "Take care of our home, take care of everything, I'll comeback, well achieved".

Latif who almost runs through the speed of the train says "Latif will be alright here; Will Sana be a perfect girl? Latif will be so good boy; Will Sana be a very good girl?"

Then, Sana blinked her eyes and the tears starting flow, train moves.

In the meantime, Waqar is still waiting outside without knowing what happened inside. Suddenly a bunch of men came in and rushed in to the Godman's room, and Eswaran guided the gang.

"Bhai, don't be worry, whatever you lost will be returned back by this moron, cops will be here in minutes" Eswaran said to Waqar.

Waqar got shocked and surprised to see Sana missing from that place, he starts searching everywhere and he could not find her.

Meanwhile, the Godman and the drunken Kumar have been arrested and taken under custody by the cops in accordance to the complaint filed by Eswaran. Waqar stood without a word and sees the Godman and Kumar are taken into the cop vehicle.

Eswaran lights up a cigarette, taps the shoulder of Waqar and leaves the place.

Then, Latif arrives to that place and sees Waqar standing stunned holding a bag with him. Latif's face is filled with guilt yet he consoles himself and approaches Waqar.

Waqar's face is so furious and he could not resist to spit the words on Sana, Latif who got angry and starts scolding Waqar.

"This is pure arrogance, you have made the mistake and curse is for Sana, right? How come almighty allows this?" said Latif.

Waqar replied, "Did she behaved like a true Muslim? She committed sin, she committed "Haraam" I tried to clean it, I attempted so many techniques even in our religion but that did not work, is that wrong to believe someone who consoled to make us heel? If so, Allah will forgive".

"First up, are you a true Muslim? you have named your daughter by the holy Quran, so in which page our holy Quran supported the practice of Darghas and these sacred threads, rose petal water, and these barbaric acts of Godman-ism?" Latif spoke with anger and tears fed in his eyes.

Waqar starred at him.

"You are a traitor and the worst follower of Islam and Prophet," said Latif.

Waqar raised his finger by indicating Latif, to stop talking and started walking away from there. Latif watches him go and the assistants of the Godman starts running away with their bags from that place.

Waqar gets back to home, Latif follows him, Khadija was preparing milk for Aisha and sees Waqar entering home angrily. Latif looks at everyone and puts his head low.

"What is wrong? Where is Sana? What happened to her? What is wrong?" shouted Khadija.

Waqar walks slowly and drinks water from the clay pot.

Latif shakes his head and said "She is missing"

Khadija's eyes blown up in shock and Aisha started shouting "Djinn, it is the one which possessed her from the sea..."

Immediately Waqar takes the clay pot from where he is drinking water, and throws it down to shut the voices of both woman and leaves that place.

Then, Latif takes a leave and Waqar comes back and calls him and said, "Hey Latif, don't think your sister is escaped, I'll kill her, I'll find and kill her".

Both Aisha and Khadija close their mouth with hands with fearing eyes.

Latif come out of the house and texted his friend Sriram, "Take care of her, I think she doesn't belong to Rameswaram anymore"

Sana watches her train crosses pamban bridge, and the sea water glittered in the setting sun from the west. Sana gave one last glace at her own island and entering the biggest Peninsula called India, geographically.

Sun slowly starts to set in Rameswaram island and she reached Mandapam. She could not find a place as the compartment is filled and seats are occupied completely.

An old woman gets in from Mandapam with a basket full of fish asks Sana for a help. She helps to place in on the above berth place for luggage. The old woman suddenly jumps over the seat and climbs to sit on the upper berth place for luggage.

Sana watched her with amusement and slowly asks her for help to climb, the old woman helped Sana to get a seat near her and train moves further from Mandpam.

Rameswaram – Chennai Egmore express is usually very accurate with its timings so it never stays exceeding its halt time in any of its stations.

Sana's nose is nearer to the fish basket of that old woman, which is so enrich and Sana cannot tolerate at one stage and further, so she asked her "When will you get down?"

The old woman replied arrogantly "Why? Are you going to lie down here? That is not the case here."

Sana looked cluelessly and the very first encounter after she eloped from her home seems to be so arrogant and unpredictable.

Slowly, her eye starts closing and she managed to sleep.

She was wake up suddenly by a sound after a small nap, asks a neighbor "Which place is this?"

"Karaikudi" the neighbor replied.

Sana is now unable to control her hunger as she is pregnant and asks the same neighbor whether the food is available there. But the train starts to move, so they insisted that the train will be halting for ten minutes at Trichy and there she can buy food.

Sana starts waiting for Trichy to arrive.

After an hour or so, she has the sensation of vomit, so she suddenly gets down from the upper tier and rushed on to the bathroom, a lady from the opposite replied that the enrichen fish smell caused that girl trouble. The old woman with the fish basket got scolded by the others and the old woman replied, "This is my business, this is how these places would be."

Sana came back and drink the water from her bottle and sat at the same place and train reached the next station.

Tiruchirapalli Junction, the train will be halting for ten more minutes here, many of the passengers gets down to get food and water bottles.

Sana gets down and bought two pieces of chappatis to eat and she had an empty water bottle so she walked some steps to fill the water bottle.

Nearer to that water filling station in the platform, an old man lied down in the bench and a pair of ear rings placed down in the platform near to him.

Many people cross by and no one bats an eye either at the old man nor at the ear rings, Sana notices that and takes that ear rings in her hand and wakes up that old man, who is Paul.

CHAPTER THIRTEEN

Back in the afternoon, when Paul left Coimbatore junction, he kept murmuring the route that Jacob told him before he boarded the train. As Paul hailed from the place where the atmospheric temperature never exceeded twenty degrees Celsius, the abrupt heat generation inside the train compartment made Paul so uncomfortable and he starts leaking out sweat heavily. Paul is talking to no one in the train, he even has been asked to have food but Paul ignored the offers.

Train travelled along through, Tirupur and Erode.

At the next station Kodumudi, a woman gets in the train carries a baby covered by a cloth and begs for money inside the compartment.

Paul, checking the ornamental characteristics of that ear ring and he really loves it, suddenly he is distracted by a woman who begs him money.

Paul keeps the ear ring in his shirt pocket, watches her and surprised to see a child inside her covered cloth, he called that lady and said "Take care of this one, aren't you aware of what you are carrying? A kid."

The beggar woman looked at Paul and said no word and moved way.

Paul receives a call from the cell phone which Jacob gave, and Paul remembers what Jacob said and he presses "green button"

Paul cannot hear properly what they speak from the other end due to the heavy noise inside the compartment, so he gets up and moves towards the door.

Heavy flow of wind again played as a barrier. He moves further towards the door by shouting over the phone. Then, Paul almost lost his grip from the door and slightly slips near the door, suddenly another train crosses parallelly, that wind heavily beats the face of Paul.

Then, he managed to take his phone and goes to bathroom, he then places his phone in his ears and asks "Who is this?".

"It is Jacob, Paul" said Jacob over the phone.

Paul replied "Yeah, yeah Jacob, I mean it's too hot here, I'm sweating my ass off." Jacob laughed from the other end and asks "Where are you? Right now,"

"In a bathroom," said Paul.

"Wait, what? What would you do there?" asks Jacob.

"Well, nothing new from what humans do, now just please tell me why you phoned me?", Paul shouted over the phone.

"Man, I just asked what was the last station you crossed" Jacob questioned.

"No, I didn't cross, the train does" replied Paul with a smile.

"Okay mate, it is time to cut the call," said Jacob.

"No no no, wait! Let me just asks someone" said Paul and leaves the bathroom and he immediately sense the train is about to stop.

He read a boarding outside the train, while holding the phone and said "Its Kulithalai, mate"

"Okay fine, in next two stops, you need to get down, next one will be Tiruchirapalli fort and the next to that is Tiruchirapalli junction, and there you have to ask a ticket for Chidambaram," said Jacob.

Paul replies, "Hmm"

"Paul. I am sorry that I'm unable to come along with you! you know right? The reservoir dam needs a better caring as there is construction work is going on day and night and I have no one to substitute," said Jacob.

"I'll take care, you please concentrate in the work" replied Paul and cuts the call.

Paul sat at the window seat and keenly watching the dark night sky and receiving the heavy wind on his face, and waiting for Trichy to come.

In some time, the train stops in a station and he found that to be Tiruchirapalli fort, and he suddenly asks the neighbor "How long will it take to reach the ect stop, that is Tiruchirapalli junction"

They replied "In five to seven minutes"

Paul suddenly takes his bag and reaches the door and stands there, he sees a huge rock decorated with lights at the top cliff and a reasonably tall church stands parallelly. In few minutes, the train stops at Tiruchirapalli junction and he gets down at Trichy.

He asks for a ticket counter and he buys a ticket for Chidambaram and enquires about the platform, they said "Platform number is, one train name is Rameswaram-Chennai Egmore express."

Paul takes a turn and mistakenly leaves the station and reaches the entrance and he is surrounded by at least ten men and each asks one,

One asks "Chennai?"

Another one asks "Do you need auto rikshaw?"

The other one asks "Do you need lodge?"

Paul got tensed and scared about these men and takes a turn and gets inside the station again and started searching the platform one, which is all the way closer to the ticket counter.

He reached the platform one and waits for the train and the time is now 22.30.

Platform one is so crowded, as the many people have been rushing for that train to Chennai.

Even though the dark night gives cool winds, the humidity level of Trichy makes Paul so uncomfortable, he starts sweating again and his shirts and hair have become so wet. Also, he is in big hunger and he wants to have food.

Due to over sweating Paul has a slight giddiness and restlessness which gives some dizzy feelings, so he slowly lied down at the bench he sat.

Th ear ring he bought for Madeline falls from the shirt pocket, he lied down and closes his eyes.

After a while, he was wakening up by a skinny brown skinned girl, who wears a half hijab which covers only head and neck, and gave his ear ring, it is Sana.

CHAPTER FOURTEEN

Sana hands over that ear ring to Paul and asks about his train, Paul replied "It will be coming from Rameswaram"

Sana then immediately pointed her train and asks Paul to show the ticket, she saw that and reconfirms with some stranger who is about to spit on platform nearby them.

Sana moves away from that stranger and calls Paul to embark inside the train as this is the train he is looking for.

Paul looks clueless and seems to be scared of seeing Sana a young girl helping him. He packs his ear ring and pouched inside his shirt. Suddenly the train horns to indicate that the train is leaving the platform. Sana urges the old Paul who is lacking concentration more often to get in the train. Finally, Paul realized himself and boards the train.

Sana finds a place beside her and the women around her feels a slight discomfort as they see Paul as an alien passenger due to his peculiar costume and highly westernized skin tone and face. Sana continuously observing Paul and his activities. Paul takes out the bible and starts reading. Sana who really wants to talk with someone feels disappointed that Paul is not ready to talk as he makes himself busy with the bible.

Then, Sana moves away from there and finds a place near the door to access more wind to blow on her face, the night breeze from the greenish lands of Thanjavur blown on Sana's face and she could feel that mysterious dark outside the door. Suddenly, a hand that touches the shoulders of Sana, she highly scared for a moment and then realized it is Paul.

Paul asks Sana to take care of her and not to stand near by the door.

Sana gives a sad and disgusting look towards Paul and asks him to go and sit in his place, Paul then sees outside through the door.

Heavy noise of engine and the extremely furious Cauvery delta's wind that blown on their face, it is completely dark outside as they could see only black outside.

"Don't you scared of this darkness outside?" asked Paul by beating the heavy engine noise and wind sound.

"I am not new to this darkness; darkness has filled my life! I have seen complete darkness followed by not even a single dot of light source; you know what Mr. Grandpa! My life is dark; hence I love this darkness," said Sana.

Paul asks "What is your age?"

"Will be turning eighteen in couple of months" replied Sana.

Paul shows a judgmental face and continues to look around.

"What do you think about this darkness?" asked Sana.

Paul took a moment and starts speaking to Sana, "Darkness is a part of life, one's life cannot be completely dark nor bright," said Paul.

"So, you have both?" asked Sana.

"I must have had every possible shade in my life," replied Paul.

Sana blinks her eyes and asks Paul "Okay! Shall we eat?"

Paul nods his head.

Sana rushed back to her seat and takes out the chapati pack and joins back Paul near the door. She also wants Paul to share the food but Paul denies.

"My name is Sana, Sana Amyra, from Rameswaram and have you been to Rameswaram?" asks Sana.

"Yeah, I've been to, but never landed my foot there" replied Paul.

"Cannot get you Mr. Grandpa" Sana asks again.

"When I was ten, I have been to Dhanushkodi via boat mail, it offered great mental peace than anything. I think it was 1957, seven years before the great cyclone, I went with my friend's family, my friend's father was working there in railways, I still remember that beach where we can easily find out lots of jelly fishes," said Paul.

Sana seems clueless as her knowledge of Dhanushkodi remains only an abandoned and lost city with shattered buildings and untouched beaches.

"My father used to take me there when I was kid, I loved being there, in fact I skipped classes and went there with my. uh! my my friend" Sana stammered and looked at Paul.

Sana remembers the days she spent with her boyfriend and the intimate memories she has with that place so she tries to change the topic as much as possible.

Paul changed his look from her and hazed outside the door, Meanwhile Sana finished the food and packs the cover and tries to throw out of door but Paul stops her and gathers the back and asks her to wait until next stop and said "You must have known this dear"

Sana closely looked at Paul who wears almost close to cowboy get up kind of outfit.

Next station, Thanjavur. Where Paul gets down from the train and throws the food waste in the pack in the garbage on the platform.

Sana seeing him running slowly like a two-year-old to the garbage and to the compartment, she did not step down from the train. Paul gets in the train and the train moves. Paul gasping as he ran for few yards, Sana did not say a word and moves away.

Paul asks her, "Why were you standing seeing me running there to find a garbage?"

"This seems so strange for me, actually I'm not this much socially responsible, like getting out of train to throw a waste, I mean I'm not that good may be," said Sana.

"You might be right but back in our place, we are strictly warned by our ancestors to keep the place clean as much as possible, because our place is made of glaciers, snows, cottages, horses, breezes, and a very small dam with enough of water to sink in our entire village but now it is happily feeding us, but yeah, we don't use plastics there in fact we are not accessible to plastics in our valley, reason is my father! He initiated it and eradicated completely, not only I am, no one in our village are accessible to plastics and we completely hate it," said Paul.

Sana looked him with excitement and replied "You belongs to a finer place I guess, May I know where is it?".

"It is located inside a small valley, name is Glenmorgan, you must have to come to Alister Wood street, everyone in the street knows who is Paul" said Paul with a proud face.

Sana giggles and said "But we are get used to these plastics, I wonder how your place is escaping from the tourists, back in Rameswaram, almost eight percentage of the workers and the businesses relying on tourism, tourists' zones are always plastic prone zones"

"So, the island of Rameswaram is up to plastic pollution?" Paul curiously asks Sana.

"It is not about only Rameswaram, and also Dhanushkodi, even the abandoned beaches are prone to plastics," said Sana.

Paul feels shocked, and asks "Dhansuhkodi too?"

"Yes, totally! See Mr. Grandpa tourists are not natives, they always treat us as the tourists' guides, they never feel that the places they visit also have to feed some number of people, Grandpa those jelly fishes you mentioned must have sunken in the oceans of plastics," said Sana.

"I never thought that Dhanushkodi would face this, I always used to tell Madeline that I love such places, I love Dhanushkodi but she never believed that I traveled on boat mail" Paul breaks down and started looking outside the door.

"Who is Madeline?" Sana asks Paul.

Paul realized later and turned at Sana after few seconds and says "Huh! We talked about our places but we did not talk about our family"

Sana now looks scared as she wants to tell all those things happened for her is he asks back about her family, she become nervous as well.

"Madeline is my wife, a painting artist, a drawing teacher, simply my lifeline," said Paul.

"Oh, where she is now?" Sana asks in a hesitant tone.

"It's you, who saved her" Paul takes out the ear ring from her pocket by saying this.

Silence between both as the heavy wind sound fills up the gap.

"Just a memory, a small simple memory of her I have as of now," said Paul.

Sana realizes that his wife is not with him now but still she seems curious to know what happened to Madeline.

"I understand but where is your wife now," asks Sana.

Paul took a second and realizes what Sana asked and said "She is there, back in my home, Glenmorgan"

Sana face glows as she concludes that Madeline is somewhere alive, Paul suddenly says "She is there inside a coffin, but alive in my paintings and in memories."

Glowing face of Sana fades and apologized him.

"This is the travel I didn't wanted to do, the travel that haunting me with its memories, uhh several years ago we used to have same type of train journeys from there Pondicherry to our place, to and fro to be exact, we had fights, we had moments, and also we made tons of love, we painted drawings, we made pancakes, and that night she gave me a pancake, that was the last night, but intimacy doesn't vary much from our first night" says Paul.

Sana giggles and hides it and asks "So now you are going to Pondicherry to see whom?"

"A place that has nothing left but the memories" replied Paul.

Sana and Paul looked at each other and Paul shows the ear ring and says "This is the last thing I bought for her in fact the same thing which I bought her for the first time, when I saw her in Pondicherry, that's why I have to get down at Chidambaram and catch Pondicherry bus."

Paul explains the whole story of him and Madeline in Pondicherry and Glenmorgan.

"I don't know I will go back to my place, there is no one awaits now other than my duty to full fill, I just need to see the place once again, where I saw her, where I was slapped by her love" says Paul.

Sana admired by his story and thinks that she deserved a love story like this, and says "Mr. Grandpa, you made me to believe again in love, the true love."

Paul closely looked at Sana and asks "Do you have a story to tell? If so please tell"

Sana stammered again and turned away from Paul and said, "Yeah, but I have always been a...been a single child a lonely person, I believed in true love just like you both, so when I saw a companion from outside, the care, the warmth, I fell for that trap, the trap men used to catch fishes like me, Mr. Grandpa I didn't have any other reason to do that, that actually happened I know that will lead to this but at that moment I felt something is working more than my brain, Mr. Grandpa, please don't be judgmental" as she says this and turned towards Paul and he is in deep sleep and didn't listened to what Sana said.

Sana delivers a very tiny smile and starts admiring how innocent, pure, and true nature of Paul's love.

Sana who almost lost belief in men's love is now just eased a bit due to Paul's nature.

In meantime, the train reaches Chidambaram and the time is almost 1.30 AM next day.

Sana sensed the station is Chidambaram and immediately wakes up Paul who is in deep sleep, she indicates that the Chidambaram has come. Both Sana and Paul are taking the pack and Paul gets down from the train and sees the Chidambaram station like a two-year-old kid watching the world. Sana who tries to wave a bye but Paul seems so distressed and clueless, Sana still standing at the footboard but her heart beats faster to help Paul, Sana still tries to call Paul to say a good bye but Paul is so distressed and he cannot even realize, that his cell phone is ringing.

Sana watches all these happening and hears the train's horn sound, she sees Paul again and he is looking at Sana with determined eyes, those eyes literally calling Sana to be with him.

Train moves.

Sana rushed back to her seat, she sat and closes her eyes.

Everyone is the platform slowly moving away, Paul still watches his compartment slowly approaching away from the platform, suddenly Sana throws her bag out and jumps out of the slowly moving train and rushed to Paul and asks him to check the call he received.

CHAPTER FIFTEEN

Sana stares at Paul, and Paul asks "What happened? Uhh, I don't know that you are also coming to Pondicherry."

Sana replied nothing and says "Shall we go? Mr. Grandpa".

Sana takes the cell phone from Paul's pocket and called Jacob, who called him few minutes ago.

Jacob speaks over the phone

"Paul, have you reached Chidambaram, where are you now?" Jacob said.

"Uhh, this is Sana" Sana replied.

Jacob over the phone shocks and panics and says "Hello! Who is this? Where is Paul, what happened to him?"

Sana calms him down and says about her "I'll be taking care of him, we are at Chidambaram, wait he is here" and she gives the phone to Paul.

Paul speaks "Yeah we are here in Chidambaram".

Jacob says "Okay who is the one talked before, is everything fine there?"

"Yeah, she is...she is..." Paul hesitates to tell who Sana is and Sana indicates in muted voice to tell her as friend but Paul cannot understand easily, so Sana takes the cell phone and says "Friend, tell everyone is Glenmorgan that Paul has a new friend now and she will be taking care of him until he reaches Pondicherry"

Jacob over the phone stays silent and said "Okay madam president".

Sana giggles and cuts the call and keeps inside her pocket.

Both leaves the railway station and hires an auto to go to Chidambaram bus stand, they both reached Chidambaram bus stand and enquires about the straight bus to Pondicherry.

Time keepers says "Wait here until 3.10 AM"

"Now the time is 1.50 AM, a solid more than one hour to go" says Sana.

"So?" asks Paul.

"Can't we just wander somewhere?" says Sana.

The mix of old and new Tamil songs filled the bus stand and the late nigh tiffin centers are also about to close in few more minutes.

Both Paul and Sana rushed into a roadside tiffin center and asked for a dosa.

The tiffin master stares at them as he is about to close the shop. He denied to offer a dosa for them as he is about to pack things.

Meanwhile, Sana acted as if she is in bugger hunger and cried to Paul and says "I have been asking you since evening and you cannot even a buy a dosa for your granddaughter who is carrying a baby inside."

Paul shocks and sees Sana.

The tiffin master looks at Sana and feels something and asks her to sit and agrees to cook a dosa for them.

Paul seeing all these activities stood stunned and eats a dosa.

Then they continued wandering the bus stand, Paul says "Hey you are a great liar, the tiffin master believed that you are pregnant."

Sana's smiling face fades and turns her look away from Paul and nods her head as she knows that she did not lie to the tiffin master.

Then, Paul and Sana go to the musical CD shop and Sana gave a glance at her favorite movie CDs inside and Paul who never known that this type of shops exists looking at those shops with excitement.

Around 3 AM, they are having badam milk in a tea shop and Paul really likes it, meanwhile the straight bus to Pondicherry via Cuddalore arrives and both Sana and Paul rushes into it to occupy better seat.

They find a two seated seat and they both argues for a window seat and both remained standing.

Every other in bus has been seated as the bus is half full but these two remained standing as no one is accepting the aisle seat as they both want the window seat.

Bus conductors comes after seeing the drama between them gives a solution, that one will be sitting near the window until Cuddalore and the other one should change after Cuddalore, so both will be having window seat experience.

This idea seems to be working for Sana and Paul but another problem arises that who will be sitting until Cuddalore.

Paul wants him to be seated and Sana half-heartedly agrees to it as she want to see the beauty of Pondicherry from the window side than seeing the path of Chidambaram to Cuddalore.

Paul takes the window seat and the Bus moves.

"Trains are always better, they have doors either side, see we were accessed to both doors and the breeze with darkness blown on our face in our train" Paul says.

Sana giggles and nods her head as the indication of accepting what Paul said.

The salt coated wind of East Coast Road blows and the Paul falls asleep, meanwhile Sana sees him and takes Paul's cell phone from her pocket and plays a snake game in it.

Bus reaches Cuddalore, Sana realizes that it is her turn for the window seat but seeing Paul fell asleep she continued to be in the aisle seat.

Conductor looks at Sana and smiles, Sana smiled back at him.

Slowly the summer dawn appears in the sky close to the sea, bus enters Pondicherry limits and proceeds further Sana wakes up by the whistle sound of conductor and sees around to confirm that the place is Pondicherry, immediately wakes up Paul and he didn't respond, Sana again shakes his shoulder and ties to wake him up but Paul didn't responded, Sana seems something fishy and tries to call conductor but before that she opens the water bottle and decides to splash water on the face of Paul but she panics as if what happens if he didn't wake up even after splashing water.

Suddenly, a bus crossed furiously next to the check post, Paul wakes up with that sound and furious wind from the window.

Sana relaxes herself and stares at Paul who asks "Oh! Is this Cuddalore? Right let us interchange our places."

Sana continued her stare.

Bus stops at bus bay in "Pudhucherry bus stand."

Paul gets down and reads the name "Pudhucherry" and says "Madeline didn't like the new name."

"So where are we heading?" asks Sana.

"We? Are you coming with me still?" asks Paul.

"Yeah, that's what I told to the one from Glenmorgan over the phone" Sana replied casually.

"So, what about your relative's house here? Aren't they would be waiting for you?" Paul asks with determination as if Sana has some relatives here in Pondicherry.

Sana giggles and says "Mr. Grandpa, when did I say I have relatives here, I came here just for you and I have to go to Chennai to meet my brother's friend, but you seemed like an infant to me my heart doesn't worked in favor of my brain to head to Chennai but yeah this is fine, I have never travelled alone anywhere, this is quite adventurous only, you don't be thinking anything unwanted, I'll be going to Chennai from here, okay now tell me, what's is the place?"

Paul scratches his white beard for few seconds and says "French colony"

Both Paul and Sana use the public wash basin to brush their tooth and goes to hire an auto rikshaw, Paul pays for the auto and they both goes to French colony.

On their way, Paul tells Sana about every place that how everything has changed since the last time he visited there.

Paul shocks to see a new park in the name of "Bharati Park" is located at the place where the art gallery was there, the place where Paul met Madeline.

"This has completely changed, I told you right, I met her in an art gallery, this is place, I'm damn sure I know this, but everything has changed, I know this road, exactly" Paul says with excitement.

Sana calmly watches him and observes his feelings and innocence.

"You do not believe me, right? Do you think I am blabbering? I know this, this road will head to Rock beach" says Paul.

Auto driver replied "Yeah, you are right."

Sana realized that Paul is right and asks auto driver to stop the auto immediately and asks Paul "Let's to the place."

Fresh morning of Pondicherry helped the flowers to bloom and the blossoms invited both Sana and Paul to the Bharathi park. Sana wandered every place and Paul sees a French warrior's statue that used to be here even before, when this place used to be art gallery.

Now Paul realizes that this is the place where both him and Madeline made their first conversation.

Instantly Paul tries to read that warrior's name again and he eventually failed to do so again, he smiles a bit and leaks some tears.

Sana watching all these actions of Paul.

Paul came to Sana and shows the statue and points the hands towards that place.

Sana understands that and she admired Paul completely by the amount of love he has in Madeline.

Sana hugs Paul and says "Mr. Grandpa, now you are not sixty-six, just go back to your age when you met Madeline".

Paul wanders around the park, the French warrior's statue seems to be talking with Paul, he tries to shake hands and the kids playing around him are laughing at them but Paul does not care about that and been mesmerized and submerged with the memories he gathered here several years ago.

Sana hazes around the park and the morning bright sun from the direction of rock beach and Paul joins her as well.

Now both starts to walk around through the streets of French colony and Paul cat quite remember the house of Madeline, and, she never told many things about her French families too, so he cannot figure out the exact location and the house.

Since most of the places are changed due to urbanization.

Both reaches Rock beach, and instantly remembers the place where he proposed.

Paul buys helium balloons and Sana asks him to write Madeline's name along with his.

Paul writes Paul – Madeline with a hear tine with Sana's pen and throws up in air, immediately Paul starts to think that Madeline is going to catch that somewhere in heaven, he keenly watches that go beyond on and on into the sea.

After the balloon has gone out of sight, Paul wants to buy another balloon and makes it fly over ocean.

Sana also buys some balloons and plays with him.

At one stage Sana gets tired of this and asks Paul to stop but he has no idea to stop, Paul must have bought almost twenty-five balloons, but he does not stop.

Then, Paul writes on the twenty sixth balloon and ready to throw in air, Sana calms him down and says "Mr. Grandpa, see your Madeline must have tired like me as of now, enough of balloons you sent." She keeps that balloon in her pocket and asks him to move from the beach but Paul still wants to be there, but Sana indicated that there so many men around seeing her as she feels embarrassing. She even looked around some men and asks Paul to move away from there.

They almost spent an entire day there, but Paul do not have heart to leave that place, he seems to be left his heart with all the balloons.

Sana guides him to shopping malls, road side street foods and the shopping bazars, but still Paul remained seeing towards the rock beach side.

"Mr. Grandpa, I'm here now, just see me" Sana asks Paul with anger.

Paul gives a short smile and "Sana...."

"Whoooooooffffffff, you called my name Mr. Grandpa! for the first time, feels good" replied Sana.

Paul smiles and Sana says "It's a nice time, you are the purest person I have seen since long time, I cannot forget this awesome trip with you the old man, Uhmm when are you leaving to Glenmorgan?"

Paul thinks for a second and says "May be tomorrow, and you are staying here, right?".

"Hmm, thousandth time I'm indicating that I need to go to Chennai" replied Sana.

"Oh, when?" Paul asks.

"In few more hours" replied Sana.

Paul face shrinks as he forgets that Sana will be leaving to Chennai.

"Where will you be staying for this night?" asks Sana.

Paul controls his tears and stammers "I.... I...uhh...I will look around here near to French colony or I just wander somewhere and will leave tomorrow".

Sana nods her head and asks him to come with her till bus stand.

"May I hire an auto?" asks Paul.

"Shall we walk?" asks Sana.

Both smiled and starts walking towards bus stand.

After reaching the bus stand, Paul reads that board "Pudhucherry bus stand" and says "Madeline hates this new name."

"Ufff, you already told it"Replies Sana.

Sana finds the Chennai bus and asks conductor for the front seat.

Paul feels empty now as Sana is leaving him now, finally Sana manages to grab front seat and waves at Paul from the window.

Paul is standing with the heavy heart at platform,

"Don't be too worried I'll be visiting Glenmorgan every month, I must know about the climate" Sana says from the bus.

Paul smiles and says "I'll be waiting for you with the pan cakes".

Sana smiled back and gets down from the bus and hugs Paul.

Now both Paul and Sana leaks tears and Sana says "Bye", suddenly Paul asks "Do you have water bottle?".

"No" says Sana.

Paul asks Sana to wait and rushes to buy water bottle and comes back to see the bus moved.

Paul disappoints and waves at the bus and leaves the bus stand slowly with heavy heart carrying the bag and the water bottle he bought.

Bus goes out of bus stand exit way slowly, suddenly a car goes past that bus swiftly and Sana's slippers were thrown out from the car in few minutes.

The gang of three kidnaped Sana from the bus stand when Paul leaves to buy the water bottle saying that old man standing near to her has fainted nearby.

They grabbed her inside the car and moved faster.

One from the gang of three said "Great work, great work dude, she is the one I saw at rock beach today"

Another one says "Nice plan buddy, that worked" and laughs.

Sana shouts heavily and another guy closes her mouth and instantly she loses conscious but subconsciously resisting what she gets.

The car goes faster in ECR towards Chennai.

The quarrel of Sana cannot be heard by the Bay of Bengal which is very closer and it had been an integral part of Sana's life since her birth.

The gang of three involved in unwanted activities that Sana never thought of experiencing.

All the worst nightmares she had right from childhood got collided together and formed into three human forms and she is seeing those right in front of her eyes.

Sana's hijab torn by her resistance but she manages to save that by holding that onto one guy's face.

Slowly she loses the conscious entirely and she faints.

One among the gang who drives car, reaches Odiyur and he wants to refresh at the rest stop nearby.

So, the car stops.

The gang of three refreshing themselves outside and one from the gang hides Sana a black cloth that used to clean the car.

All three were smoking near the tea shop.

Heavy volume of the music speakers that playing old nineties Tamil songs helped Sana to regain her consciousness.

Sana gets down from the car silently, she makes over that black cloth over the beat seat to fool them then, the song changes to "Innisai paadi varum". Sana runs and searches the bus to Chennai, but she cannot find one but she sees that the gang of three realizes that Sana is missing. So, she immediately gets in the Chennai – Pondicherry bus and hides behind a huge travel bag, which is Gautam's.

CHAPTER SIXTEEN

Gautam listened to the last two days story of Sana right from eloping from Rameswaram to hiding behind Gautam's travel bag. Sana didn't talk about her pregnancy and the issues happened at Rameswaram. All three, Sana, Gautam and Lurdhu are looking at each other.

Sana says "My entrance exam is nearing, I must go to Chennai, my brother's friend is waiting for me, I think he must have informed to my brother, I don't know what is happening back in Rameswaram"

"Your helping tendency and innocence to help others has put yourself in trouble" says Lurdhu.

"No anna, the masculinity and urge to show their masculinity towards a girl has made that gang of three do this" says Gautam.

"Anna people says that the westernized modern dresses that shows skins is the reason for men to get tempted and do these kinds of activities but in what case does her hijab failed to hide her skin?" asks Gautam.

Lurdhu nods his head and sees Sana's torn hijab scarf in around her neck.

Gautam looks around to confirm that the conductor has slept and asks Sana to come out and asks her to take rest and sleep in the next seat.

The couples whom created problems earlier also had slept and the entire bus in silence expect the wind that blows in.

Gautam notices Sana's wounds and promises her to buy medicines tomorrow in Pondicherry, "I'll send you to Chennai, now take rest"

Sana says "It is very hard for me to believe men around me, but I don't have an option".

"That is a fair disbelief, I'm sorry" says Gautam.

Lurdhu smiles at Gautam and asks him to sit with him.

"Life is not stable for anyone, right?" asks Lurdhu.

"I'm not sure anna, but I would say, Life is logicless and meaningless, and I feel everything is comprised of social animal's emotions and mind hoax" says Gautam.

Lurdhu smiles and Gautam asks "What is your plan tomorrow? Where are you going?".

Lurdhu takes out a visiting card and gives to Gautam, it was written "Moon light boarding and lodging, Kurichikuppam, Pondicherry"

"Who is here?" asks Gautam.

"I told you, right? Sundaram has borrowed forty-five thousand from me for the puberty function of her daughter, Akhila" says Lurdhu.

Gautam nods his head as saying "yes"

"I went to his home next day to greet her daughter, but his wife Rani said that Akhila has hit her puberty seven months ago" says Lurdhu.

Lurdhu continues his story, as Sundaram's first wife Rani has said that he must have bought the money for Shanthi, the second wife of Sundaram and she also complained to him as Shanthi almost looted Sundaram's income.

Lurdhu then, leaves the place and asks Rani to help to find Sundaram. Lurdhu then realized that he has been betrayed and fooled by Sundaram. Even after fifteen days

Sundaram is still missing from the city and he cannot find him anywhere. Lurdhu's share auto also been seized due to irregular due amount paid to the finance company where he bought the auto.

Lurdhu is under severe financial crisis and eventually he has lost his saving too to Sundaram. Few days later, a postal letter came to his house. That was from his children's school, denoting that, tuition fees must be paid for the next academic year. Lurdhu got tensed and shattered that he lost the money to Sundaram and now he is unable to pay the fee for his children's education.

Immediately he decides to go to Amjinkarai where Shanthi's house is located. Lurdhu finds that Shanthi's house is locked, he enquires the neighbors but no one is aware of where she is.

Only one from the neighbor said, that Shanthi's brother will be roaming near Arumbakkam to Nsk nagar bus stop with Apache bike, whose name is Siva.

Lurdhu asks a little boy who is playing in the road about Siva, the little boy cursed Siva as he is one of the drunkard morons in their hood, he always used to be high and the boy opened up a new thing, that Siva has bought a new bike that is Apache bike.

Lurdhu now realizes that Sundaram looted money from him just to buy a new bike for Shanthi's brother, Lurdhu calls that little boy with him just to identify Siva in Arumbakkam.

Both searched for Siva but could not find him, later the little boy said that he would be in wine shop bar. Immediately both Lurdhu and the little boy rushed to the nearby wineshop bar.

The little boy finds out the white Apache bike parked outside the bar is his, he also guessed that Siva will be drinking inside the wine shop bar.

Lurdhu thanked the little boy then entered the wine shop and shouted "a new white Apache bike is stolen".

No one bats an eye expect one who is Siva, who rushed outside and made sure that his bike is fine, he came back inside to see Lurdhu is sitting next to his place.

Lurdhu slowly starts the conversation by complimenting about the bike and then complimenting his looks, he also decided to spend the very little money he has, on Siva's drinks. Lurdhu decided that by making Siva drunk he can gather information about her sister and Sundaram.

Siva starts getting higher and higher slowly and he starts to believe Lurdhu as his friend as he buys whatever Siva wants in that wine shop.

After some rounds of consuming alcohol, Siva starts blabbering about his past love and spits some words about the persons he hates in his life, Lurdhu were tolerating all these and keenly watched him as he needed more information from him about his sister Shanthi and her husband Sundaram. Lurdhu slowly asked about the new Apache bike he got, Siva smiled and opened up about his brother-in-law, Sundaram.

"My brother-in-law is my asset, he works in an ice exchange factory at harbor, but that is what his social status says" Siva talked about Sundaram to Lurdhu.

"Oh," Lurdhu listened to Siva as if he did not know anything about Sundaram.

"He has spent thousands and lakhs for me and my sister, ever since the day she got married, in fact right from the day their relationship started," said Siva.

"Fine, but how come a simple factor worker managed to spend this much for you both?" asked Lurdhu.

Siva blinks his eyes, and asked Lurdhu to come forward and said in a husky voice "Factory worker is just said for his social status, do you know what he works for?"

Lurdhu listened to him curiously.

"Aquatic cocaine, almost sixty to seventy agents were serving from Chennai, the greatest underground mafia yet the most under spoken one in the narcotics department, Sundaram has been the part of this ever since he joined to this job, he has been easily influenced by the dealers as he is money minded," said Siva.

"Aquatic Cocaine?" Lurdhu asked curiously.

"Frozen fish, since Chennai fishing harbor exchanges enormous amount ice to keep fish frozen, several agents revolve around harbor to catch the deal, Frozen fish are filled with cocaine bladders inside and the ice factory agents were used to fill, re fill and also to transit the frozen fishes, and the king of all agents is none other than my brother-in-law, Sundaram but he acts like he has nothing to deal with, that's how he earns money and I got my brand-new bike," said Siva.

Lurdhu shocked and his reactions says that he cannot believe that Sundaram has hidden this illegal and unethical activity from everyone around him. Lurdhu further asked "So where is your big-B, I mean your brother-in-law?"

"Entire Chennai city and its surroundings receive cocaine from Mexico drug dealers' ship containers, seven years ago Chennai harbor has stopped the Mexico export trades due to over taxation issues, since then Pondicherry has become the transit hub, due to over restrictions by road and sea, the distribution and the transportation of cocaine has become tough, so the dealers hired one of the agents to transit the cocaine from Pondicherry to Chennai. Sundaram has planned to hide the cocaine bladder filled frozen fishes separately from the check post, so he went to Pondicherry" said Siva and almost flattered.

But Lurdhu tried to wake him up to know about the exact location in Pondicherry but Siva reached sky high and he is completely flattered.

Lurdhu searched his pocket and found a visiting card, which is written "Moon light boarding and lodging, Kurichikuppam, Pondicherry."

"Then I drank the last bottle I bought for him and took this bus" says Lurdhu.

Gautam's eye ball forgets to move and blink after listening about Sundaram's story. Lurdhu yawns then he turns around and sees Sana who is still in deep sleep.

It is early morning just before dawn, bus enters Pondicherry limit.

Gautam receives the SMS from "Rent a resort" that the cottage is ready to check in. Bus reaches bus stand, and immediately Gautam wakes up Sana and ask her be ready to go.

Sana wakes up and scratches her stomach and spits out from the bus, wipes the mouth, and asks for some water to Gautam. Bus stops and both Gautam and Lurdhu giving signals to each other and starts staring at the bus conductor.

Conductor also stares back at them, but he cannot last long, he becomes uncomfortable but both Gautam and Lurdhu did not stop staring meanwhile when the stare competition is happening Sana managed to get down from the bus. Suddenly both Gautam and Lurdhu stopped staring and gets down from the bus.

The crazy couples are also gets down and they both looked at Sana and makes her discomfort, Gautam stares again at them and made them go away from there.

Sana still scratches her stomach; Gautam sees and asks her "Are you hungry?". Without waiting for Sana's answer Gautam orders three tea in a nearby tea stall and serves it to Sana.

Soon after, all three hires an auto and reaches the "Rent a resort" cottage house which is close to the sea.

All three enters the resort and Gautam wakes up the sleeping watchman to call the receptionist. Then they enter inside.

Gautam shows the SMS to confirm and he filled the details of all three and he mentioned Sana as Vaithegi, his mother's name as he don't want Sana's original identity to be revealed anywhere as she is yet to turn eighteen, he signals Lurdhu and says "I know it is illegal but I have to do this for her safety" and signed the documents to rent a resort there, meanwhile Lurdhu is feeling shy as he had never been to this type of place before and her face tells that he is uncomfortable and Gautam notices that and he holds the hands in manner to tell "Nothing to worry, be cool".

Sana still did not get out of the nightmares she faced last night, and she seen biting her nails and standing. Gautam receives the key from the receptionist and then the watchman guides them to the cottage at shore. On their way the watchman lectures about the beauty and heritage of this place, as he speaks the dawn slowly appears and Sana hazed at it and remembers her day similarly starts at Rameswaram.

They reached the cottage, has a front resting area made of bamboo trees, and a hall with fully air-conditioned facility, a room with attached bathroom and a kitchen, then a backyard where there is another external bathroom.

Gautam tipped the watchman, and let him go. Gautam asks Lurdhu "When are we going anna?" Lurdhu looks at him with hesitation and shows his discomfort being there. Gautam says "Does it seems good to take a girl to such place?"

Lurdhu shakes head, Gautam asks Lurdhu to change the shirt, Lurdhu says "I don't bring any"

Gautam immediately says "Anna, I have a shirt for you, I hanged in the hanger inside, please go and wear" Lurdhu hesitated initially but agreed to wear his shirt.

Lurdhu wears Gautam's blue formal shirt and walks out of the cottage with pride, Gautam appreciates his look and asks him to get ready.

Gautam tells Sana "Sana, don't be worried everything will be okay, I'll send you to Chennai and also we will find a way to find your bag, hmm if my guess is correct, I think as of now it will be handed over to the CMBT police hub as unattended bags from the buses goes there, so believe me wait here for some time, we will finish one job and will be right back"

Sana sits down and scratches her stomach and Gautam indicates calls the attender to deliver breakfast for the cottage. The sea breeze and sound of waves alongside the morning light hearted heat surrounded the place. Sana agreed to stay and both Gautam and Lurdhu gets ready to go to "Moon light boarding and lodging, Kurichikuppam, Pondicherry". They ask about the place to the watchman; he mentions that the place is approximately two kilo meters from here.

Gautam and Lurdhu marches towards "Moon light boarding and lodging" to Kurichikuppam. Gautam greets the receptionist and asks about Sundaram.

Receptionist denies that no one named Sundaram has checked in. Both Gautam and Lurdhu face each other and whistled to call the cops along with the customs officers.

On their way, Gautam informed the local cops and the narcotics bureau, they surrounded the Moon light lodge, and they are all in readiness to catch the culprit. Receptionist starts shouting and the cops pulled him down to surrender.

Cops can find the room number two hundred and five is Sundaram's, through the unregistered ledger that used in the lodge and the cops asks the room boy to go call him and make him open the door to re confirm Sundaram's presence.

The room boy carries the tea serving plate and knocks the door of room number two-zero-five. Sundaram opens and rejects the room boy and tries to close the door but the room boy has fixed the resistor in the room's door gap in order that Sundaram cannot close the door instantly, in meantime, the surrounded cops entered Sundaram's room and seized the packets of cocaine bladders that he smuggled in all these days he stayed in Pondicherry.

Sundaram tries to escape from the cops but he is firmly surrounded by the cops, while the cops filled the room and got Sundaram arrested, a person calmy opens the bathroom without any hurry and the person is in her bath suite who kept her eyes closed with soap and says "Hey, make me find you"

Every cop calmly watches her doing all these stuffs, and Sundaram then shouted "Shanthiiiii", and she immediately cleared her eyes and shocked to see the cops around her.

Cops gathered the cocaine bladders from there and ordered to file a complaint against the lodge. They are taking way Sundaram under custody.

At downstairs, both Gautam and Lurdhu are standing, Sundaram shocked to see Lurdhu here.

Gautam handles the verified documents of evidences and the witness that told Lurdhu about Sundaram, Shanthi's brother.

Cops also came to know that, there are lots of aquatic cocaine bladders have been selling illegally by several goons in and around Pondicherry. Press and media are rushed to this place after knowing about the police action of seizing bulk of cocaine powders.

Cops are attending the press and a cop, who is head of operation says "People need not be worries, we almost got the trump card of this smuggling, now we ensure that the Pondicherry is completely cocaine free, lastly three men from Chennai have bought cocaine from the accused we arrested now, as the master source is caught, we can expect the local goons come out and show their heads to us, thank you".

Meanwhile, in between the press meet, Sundaram have been locked in the police jeep and Lurdhu is talking to him. Sundaram has no words to say to Lurdhu as he feels guilty, Lurdhu says "It is not my intention to trap you, what I needed is my forty five thousand you borrowed from me, my children needs their father's money to study, oh sorry their mother's money to study, yeah, you must have known it is her money, she deposited in the post office for her children's study but I gave you that money because you asked it for your daughter, that much I care for your daughter, you looted my entire savings just to buy another luxurious bike for your brother in law, let the truth wins".

Sundaram listened to all did not spoke a word and looked at Gautam with determination as if he will be taking revenge once he cleared out from the case.

Gautam warns Sundaram as to not to think of that, but Sundaram continued his determined stare at Gautam.

After finishing the press meet, the cops taken Sundaram to their station under their custody, Lurdhu watches him go and both Gautam and Lurdhu starts to walk.

Lurdhu says “I think, it’s time that I need to go back, and see my work”.

“Anna, do you really think, it is the time?” Gautam asks.

“My boys would be waiting, I don’t know about the future of them in education, I don’t know how I will be paying their school fees, the culprit would be returned me the money” says Paul.

“Anna, can you? Can you please check your shirt pocket?” asks Gautam.

Lurdhu checks his shirt pocket, he finds nothing and Gautam asks him to check the inner pocket. Lurdhu take out a cheque from his inner pocket which was signed by Gautam and the cost written on it indicates that it is fifty thousand rupees cheque.

Lurdhu looking at Gautam cluelessly with a shock, he then understands that Gautam gifted him the money.

“That’s all I can afford as of now anna” says Gautam.

Lurdhu slightly leak out some tears and breaks down emotionally.

Gautam immediately hugged him and says “Take care of everyone around you, your children need education more than anything, only that will come until last, one’s proper education will save one’s entire generation, that is what I believe.”

Lurdhu nods his head as the sign of agreeing with Gautam and says “Thank you so much, you have saved my problems which I can never dreamt of solving this much easy.”

"Lurdhu na, solving a problem is as easy as anything, I will tell you one thing, physically clouds have nothing to do with hiding the sun, but philosophically clouds actually pretends to be hiding the sun from us, but you see that actually works, whenever the cloud hides the sun the intensity of heat reduces, that is how you should think, you can hide your problems with a simple solution first and it can eventually lead to solving the problem."

Words of Gautam energizes Lurdhu and got motivated, they both reached the railway station, Lurdhu buys ticket for Chennai, and hugs Gautam and cries out loudly, Gautam also feels emotional.

Lurdhu asks the phone number of Gautam and asks him to contact him once, reaching Chennai.

Gautam sends off Lurdhu in the train and waves his hand until Lurdhu is visible to him. Lurdhu leaves to Chennai.

Gautam hires the auto and reaches rent a resort, and goes to his cottage.

He calls Sana, and she is missing from the hall, kitchen and at the backyard, he the opens the room and shocked to see Sana lying fainted in her bed with full of blood in her lower part of the body.

Gautam shocked to see Sana's situation as he was not aware of anything what Sana going through.

CHAPTER SEVENTEEN

A day before morning in Rameswaram, Latif receives a call from Sriram that Sana have not reached either contacted Sriram in Chennai. Latif has no idea about what would have happened to Sana on her way to Chennai and he got literally sad about the news he received about Sana. He and finished all his morning regular prayer duties and reached Sana's house with hurry and he completely looked tensed. All lights were on inside their house even at the bright morning sun shines outside.

Two heavy sedans were also parked outside Sana's home and several new chappals are also found outside their door, Latif senses that there are so many new persons filled the house. He enters inside and hears a crying voice of Khadija and sees so many new men in traditional Islamic outfits. Latif scares about the situation and Khadija's crying then he rushed into Waqar's room thinking that something has happened to Waqar, but instantly calmed down to see Waqar been consoled by two men of same age of Waqar's, suddenly he thought something would have happened to Aisha, then he rushed to her room and starts crying heavily, suddenly he received a heavy blow on his head from Aisha.

"I should enter after life, after you, bloody idiot" said Aisha with full of anger.

Latif calmed himself down and came out of the room to see two men who were consoling Waqar is now starts to leave by saying "We ensure that almost every man from Keezhakarai is responsible for Sana's safety and we will send our boys to every corner of Tamil Nadu, Allah saves you"

Latif faces shrinks in sadness and fear, his hands were shaking as if he was in a snow world meanwhile, he received the next call from Sriram.

"Latif, better don't waste time, a slight delay might cost her life so file a complaint as soon as possible, the poor girl must see her life" said Sriram over the phone. Latif cries inside with guilt along with fear and prays to God.

A day passed.

Next day morning, a young man who is one of the neighbors of them rushing to Waqar's home and asks him to turn on the TV and switch to news channel, saying "Sana, Sana, Sana"

Immediately Waqar switched on the TV after long time, he switches to news channel as well, but the newsreader currently reading about the trending cinema news, the young man who just came from the neighborhood asks them to wait for turn of that news. Khadija and Aisha are also rushed to hall and watches TV.

Waqar feels uncomfortable as he is not the man who watches cinema and he hates the cinema industry but now he is forced to watch the news.

"Actor A declines the marriage rumors with actress B, but partially agrees his relationship with actress C" the news rolls on the TV.

Waqar feels more uncomfortable and turn this head towards east and west to keep his eyes and ears away from TV.

After sometime, the young man calls him and shows, "SSLC and JEE hallticket of a girl is found missing in a bus at

Chennai CMBT, the unattended bag that was found earlier this morning is claimed by the police and they came to know that the bag belongs to a girl named Sana Amyra and she belongs to Rameswaram...."

Waqar faces Khadija and Aisha and instantly calls the men from Keezhakarai, at the same time Latif also rushes to Waqar's house after knowing about the news. Waqar scolds about Sana generally to Latif and says "I'll find soon to kill her"

Latif is shocked by the words of Waqar, he become tensed and confused about the situation of Sana right now in Chennai. He also called Sriram instantly and told the news, Sriram agrees to search Sana as soon as possible.

The same news flashed in a hospital outpatient block's TV and literally no one bats an eye towards the news. In the same hospital's medical shop, Gautam buys the glucose bottle along with the needles and syringe that used for IV.

Gautam enters the ward and Sana is sleeping on a bed with the hospital dress that is usually given for patients and she has been admitted for the heavy loss of blood from her body, glucose has been given for her internally. Gautam came to know that Sana got aborted from the doctor's report.

He asked the doctor about her condition, Doctor said that she is completely fine but her baby got aborted due to some unwanted mishandlings happened and stating that is common, and consoled Gautam thinking that he is the husband of the girl.

Gautam realizes that the last night's incident might have made this, the gang whom abused Sana is responsible for this. He rubs his face and enters the ward to see Sana wakes up and cries loudly about what happened, Gautam cannot control tears and goes close to Sana and he quite cannot control her tears.

Gautam tries to say “Sana, okay this too shall pass.”

Sana suddenly slaps Gautam and screams “What passed is my baby, scoundrel.”

Nurse enters the ward and asks Sana to keep quiet and but she did not care about that still screams more, Nurse says “Girl, stop screaming, it is of no use, you both must have controlled your sexual desire at least for few months, now see what costed you?”

Sana screams more and more after listening to her, and Gautam asks the nurse to leave and he ensure to take care of Sana.

Gautam again goes to Sana who is still crying and wipes her tears away with his hand and Sana immediately rests her head on Gautam’s chest and cries more.

The entire hospital receives the loud scream of Sana and it slowly faded away in quite some time. Sana sleeps in the bed and Gautam takes the floor as bed and spend their night at hospital.

Next day morning, Sana got discharged, she now changes to her dress and wears the hijab around her neck and the nurse asks suddenly “Is this a love marriage?”, both Sana and Gautam looked at each other and Gautam replies “People do love for marriage and people do marriages for love, but in what case, these love and marriages are separated and united?”. Nurse leaves the place immediately.

Gautam assists Sana and he also buys the prescribed medicines from the medical shop and comes out of the hospital. He hires an auto and asks Sana “Shall we go? May I talk to your brother and explain the situation?”. Sana replied nothing and Gautam slowly helps her to get into the auto.

They both reaches the cottage Gautam booked yesterday morning and opens the room and asks Sana to take rest there, the sound of waves and the blow of winds consistently breaks the silence between them, Sana's ever glowing face is now filled with all the dullness in the world and her face now indicates the definition of sadness and then Gautam says "I have the habit of taking bath after visiting hospital, so please spare me a minute." He goes to the bathroom.

After bathing he comes out and he finds Sana missing in the cottage and he searches around here and there but she seems to be missing from there, he instantly runs outside to call the watchman and he finds Sana near the shore, so he run towards her shouting her name.

Sana is travelling inside her best friend "Bay of Bengal" beating the waves. She chooses to die by getting inside her friend which has been an integral part of her life since her birth, but her friend stops her by resisting her by sending waves heavily. Sana slowed down a bit due to the heavy and huge waves from the sea. In meantime, she struggling against the waves, Gautam comes in for rescue and he grabs her and pulled her away, the outrageous waves helped Sana to reach the shore.

Gautam then relaxes himself and scolds Sana,

"How foolish you are? I though you are brave girl" Gautam says and gasps.

Sana replied nothing and starts crying again, the cottage watchman came and he starts quarrelling with Gautam and Sana as if someone dies inside the premises of Rent a resort property, he should answer to the judicial and, he must be fired. The watchman got furious and throws away the bag of Gautam and asks both to leave immediately and, Gautam denies and he asks him to repay the money he paid in the morning but the watchman threatens to file a complaint against him denoting that they both attempted suicide in our premises.

"Premises? Has your owner entirely bought the Bay of Bengal right from Bangladesh to Palk straight? Do you think I skipped Geography classes?" asks Gautam to the watchman.

But the watchman tries to call the police and Sana panicked of the situation, Gautam realizes and accepts to leave the cottage. Gautam asks Sana to leave from there and he finally requested the watchman as he wants to talk with the receptionist girl who talked through phone to make him book this cottage. The watchman allowed him to do, Sana is waiting for him at the gate.

Gautam goes to that receptionist and says "Hi, is this the landline phone that you called me, right?"

"Yeah sir, I use this phone to call everyone who registers," says the receptionist.

"Thank you for everything my life wouldn't have faced this much adventurous without your call through this phone, keep inspiring and keep people meet adventures more, take care of your lipstick I guess you buy one for a day, bye" Gautam spoke with the receptionist and leaves slowly.

Watchman seeing him go and Gautam asks Sana to move forward, they both leaves the front gate and immediately a loud shout arouses from inside the resort, and both Gautam and Sana start running quickly. They both have been followed by the watchman who is holding the cut off landline phone wire along with the phone which was cut by Gautam.

They both hires an auto suddenly and Sana smiled a bit, Gautam sees that and he asks "Did you smile?"

Sana kept quit for a minute and Gautam says "I have seen the flower bloom for the first time,"

They both entered the city and Gautam takes Sana to a textile shop, and asks her change to the new outfit as she do not have a spare, also the dress she is currently wearing is completely wet. Sana fears about everything she sees.

Gautam pleaded Sana to buy a new dress, Sana is genuinely confused to buy a dress as she never selected a dress in her entire life.

Sana finally chooses a long kurti top and a jean, she asks for a trial room and she finds it. Sana removes her dress and she finds something in her pocket. She takes out to see that is the cell phone of Paul and his ear rings. She realizes that she forgot to give him both, and the cell phone is not working as the sea water entered it, she changed to long kurti top and jean, then she takes the hijab scarf with her to tie around her neck but she thinks for a second and unties it and leaves it there in trial room.

Gautam paid the bill, and Sana feels guilty of making Gautam paying all the bills for her, and she promises him to repay the debts that he spent right after she starts working. Gautam accepts with a smile and says "So, for that you need to sink in with education not with Indian ocean".

"But that was Bay of Bengal" replied Sana.

"I know but I said it to match the rhyme" Gautam says.

Sana now reminds him about Paul and his cellphone stuck with her and, she talks about the importance of these ear rings. Sana then says "We must find him and handover this must"

Gautam asks "Fine, but where could we find him, and are you sure? Is he in Pondicherry still?"

"Paul said that, he will be leaving tomorrow or by this evening," said Sana.

Gautam smiles and says "Let's search."

Sana and Gautam revolve the entire bazar streets, bus stands, and some more streets and searches Paul. They searched in churches, and in ashrams.

Then, Sana guides Gautam to the French colony and they roam in every street corner and they could not find Paul. Sana feels so tired as she is still in medications and just came out of hospital, Gautam asks Sana to stop searching him but Sana refuses and says "I will tell you another place, Bharati Park."

Both goes to Bharati Park and they search him near the French warrior statue and Sana fails to find him, it is almost afternoon, Sana had the final option of looking for him in the beach. They both then goes to beach, through the auto.

On nearing the rock beach, Sana looks up towards the sky and her eye pupil goes big and Gautam also looks up, they get down from the auto.

They both see numerous helium balloons flying up in the blue sky and they never really care about the blue waters down there. But a man who enjoys a healthy economic growth of selling helium balloons to a single person for two days is sitting happily and eats ice cream.

Sana came closely and taps the shoulder of man, who launched the helium balloons up in the sky and calls "Mr. Grandpa".

It is Paul and he gets excited to Sana back to him. Sana leaks out tears and hugs Paul, and Gautam looking at them and smiles.

CHAPTER EIGHTEEN

Sana gave the ear ring to Paul, and asks "Have you forgot?". Paul opens the ring packet and says "This is what I have been asking to Madeline since you left, but why you went without waiting for me, I said right? I will buy a water bottle for you?"

Sana looks at Gautam and smiles, then she realized and introduces Gautam to Paul. Paul and Gautam looking at each other and Paul mistakenly understands that Gautam would be her lover. Nevertheless, he asks Gautam "How long you both are in love?"

Both Sana and Gautam simultaneously say "No"

Paul shocks about the instance denying of both, and asks them to wait for a minute and started walking towards the sea, meanwhile the balloon seller asks for another one to Paul and Paul replied "No, wait" and walks towards the sea.

As both Sana and Gautam are watching him, he throws the ear ring up but it fell instantly, then he tries again and it fell again. Gautam who understands his feeling as he wants to send it to Madeline, he runs towards him and asks him spare him a minute.

"Mr. Paul, believe me, I'll help you to reach this stud to Madeline," said Gautam.

"It is not stud; it is an ear ring I bought for Madeline" replied Paul with a strong voice.

Gautam smiles and says "Yeah, I know, but you bought it for Madeline, right? Not for Bay of Bengal I guess, so let me do one thing, put this pair of ear rings inside the balloon and send it to Madeline up there, after you sent the balloon with ear rings you cannot send another one there, that is the indication of your Madeline accepted your gift, believe me, and try once."

Paul stares at Gautam and feels hesitant to give the ear rings to him, he also looks at Sana and signs with eyes as the indication of seeking belief on Gautam.

Sana watches all these and signs to indicate that she is okay with Gautam. Then, Paul gives the ear rings to Gautam but still with the slight hesitation. Gautam now buys two helium balloons from the seller and puts in the ear ring in one and fills it with regular helium gas in it. Then, he gives the balloon in the hands of Paul and asks him to make it fly in the air.

Paul receives the balloon from Gautam and throws it in air, but after a fraction of second Paul grabs the balloon again with both his palm then he closes the eyes and kisses the balloon thinking of kissing Madeline's forehead and slowly released the hands, the balloon flies away in the air slowly and both Sana and Gautam watch it go, Paul then slowly opened his eyes and immediately shrink the eyes as he looks up to see the balloon going up in the sunshine.

In meantime, as Paul is looking above towards the sky, Gautam fills the other balloon with sand and asks the balloon seller to fil it with the normal gas.

The seller initially hesitated as his business would end with Paul, Gautam forced him as he had done enough of business with Paul for past two days. The seller fills balloon with the normal air which also consists of some sand. Gautam gives the balloon and says "Mr. Paul, Madeline might have received your ear rings so she must be settled somewhere in heaven now, so it is tough for her to catch the other balloon now, so shall we try?"

Paul receives the balloon and tries to fly it in air but the balloon miserably fails to fly and Paul tries again and again but the balloon filled with normal air does not go up as much higher as helium gas balloons. The balloon drops and drops and drops further which makes Paul believe Gautam. He turns towards Gautam and looks at him and controls the smiles which Gautam noted and says "Don't try to hide smile Mr. Paul, Smile is the best ingredient for whatever you do". Paul then smiles slowly and Sana watches all these dramas by Gautam silently.

Gautam came to Sana and says "He is happy now"

Sana asks "Is he mentally unstable?"

"I don't think so, he is stable than we both, yeah his mind is constantly innocent and unlike us who were claimed to be mentally stable"

Sana stays silent, and asks Paul to leave the beach. The balloon seller comes and hugs Paul and tells Sana "He is being here for two day, he slept on the bench, I use to sell balloons here for past four to five years, no one really cared about me during all these days but this man cared about my health, my family and also about my career, don't think I will just lose my business, I will the man who cared for me in my life after a very long time, in fact I gave him balloons for free today".

Paul hugs him back and gave a tap on his shoulders and says "Try to become a successful balloon businessman"

The seller laughs and leaks tears simultaneously.

Gautam is so impressed with the character of Paul and thinks that the adventures he faced in last two days has led him to the most adventurous man ever. Gautam asks Sana

"Tell me, Is he mentally unstable?"

Sana shakes her head.

He also guides Paul on their way to hotel to have lunch.

All three, Paul, Sana and Gautam are having lunch at a French café, and in mid of meal, Sana says "Please make a note of whatever you spend for me, I'll repay soon". Paul looks at Sana and continues to eat.

Meanwhile in Chennai, Sriram rushed onto CMBT police station where Sana's bag is taken under custody as the unattended bag. Sriram claims that bag is her sister's and the cops suspect him as he has the Hindu name and her sister has an Islamic name. Cops cross questioned Sriram, and Sriram tells that she is his friend's sister and she eloped from her house two days before.

Cops from that station get alerted and immediately calls Rameswaram Police control room and enquires about that is there any missing case found in their limits.

They replied "No"

But thc Rameswaram police rushed to Sana's place and they began the enquiry at their home.

Waqar, Khadija and Aisha are enquired by the cops and Waqar tells "Sir, thanks for the concern but I have sent my men to Chennai to get my daughter, they will take care of the issue and I did not even file a complaint to you".

Aisha starts scolding Sana again as she spoiled their family's name and the cops returned to station to reply to the query asked from the CMBT police station, Chennai.

Cops at the CMBT station looks worried as Sana's family is not obeying with cops, and the media attention is also peaking rightly as this is issue of a seventeen-year-old.

Cops the addresses the media by saying, "The girl's family contacted us and they are on their way to collect the certificates and the bag"

Then, they also ordered Sriram to call his friend Latif.

Latif, who is half mindedly working at the shop, received the call and Sriram urges him to come to Chennai immediately. Latif then closes the shop and rushes to Sana's home.

Waqar shocked on seeing Latif and asked "What about the shop?"

"I closed it," said Latif.

Waqar argues with Latif for closing the shop without his knowledge.

Latif says "Yeah, it is your shop, I have no right to close it without your knowledge, because it is your property"

Waqar stay silent, "But what about your daughter? She is Sana, not Sana electronics, she is not a property, she is a human with blood, flesh, and emotions, you cannot deal her like a property you owned"

"Latif, it is too late to speak, you know what she had done, is that our prophet said?" Waqar asks with anger.

"No, but what are all you have done are also not prescribed by prophet" Latif replied in a sarcastic tone.

Waqar looks at Khadija and Aisha, "You believed in the practices of tying up sacred threads, you believed in rose petal filled water bottle" says Latif and giggles in sarcastic tone again.

Waqar gets angry in him and called his name loudly, "Is that? ...is that? The Zam Zam holy water? Isn't, it is just a local water from tap and you believed in it, there is no other water in the world is as holy as Zam Zam water, now tell me who is against Islam and just rethink who is against Islam, I bet Allah won't spare your mistakes", Latif threatens with anger and Waqar quietly listens with confusion.

"And finally, our holy Qurran haven't said anything about killing your own daughter for the family pride, it is completely satanic, Mr. Abdul Waqar" said Latif and Aisha starts scolding Latif, "You called his name, you are a satan, idiot, do you think whom you are standing against? The man who gave life to you, without him you are just a poor beggar, oh wait! You are still a beggar, who are you to deal our family problems? Are you part of our family? Who are you?"

Latif then realizes that he is just a worker in their shop and he has no right to ask about their family issues, he leaked tears and hides it with smile and leaves.

Khadija seems worried and Waqar shaken by the words of both Latif and Aisha.

"I may have no real connection with the family, but everyone knows what is up with me and Sana, I literally seen her as my sister, I had her in my hands when she was born, I know how precious she was to this family, I still remember how you both named her with extreme joy, and I need to go and save her, I need to care for my Sana's future" Latif said with tears along with smile and leaves.

Waqar and Khadija looked at each other.

Latif took his bag and went to railway station and board the train to Chennai, he prayed to the god after sitting in the seat and immediately calls Sriram.

Sriram picks up the call and Latif speaks over the phone, "I'm coming to Chennai". Sriram informs this to the cops and they still tell Sriram to wait in the station but his friends rushed to the police station with the help of the big shot in their area.

Cops agreed to leave Sriram, but asked him not to leave the city and to get Latif to claim the certificates and Sana's family.

In between all the hurries that happened at Rameswaram and Chennai, all three Paul, Sana and Gautam came out and walks a bit with the help of trees' shadows.

Paul breaks the silence by asking both "I need to go back home"

Both Sana and Gautam looked at Paul and Paul says "I have lot of works to do, I came here to see what Madeline wanted to see and I also sent the ear ring to her, it is time for me to go back to work, I should rejoin to the duty"

Gautam and Sana stay speechless as they do not know what to say, as they understand that Paul must leave but also, they started loving Paul more and more and they cannot leave him.

"Shall I come and join with you in Glenmorgan?" asks Sana.

Gautam stares at Sana suddenly and says "Do you remember that you lost your certificates? We need to find it and you must reach your brother's friend place".

Sana puts her head down and starts beings so sad and Paul says "No, you guys must have some work, but I need to go and will surely miss everyone I met here, and especially you little girl".

Both Gautam and Sana smiles, and Paul says "Every time whenever I come to Pondicherry, this place has been giving me the best persons of my life".

Sana tells about the cell phone of Paul as it is not working, she says "We need to tell Jacob about your coming for that we need to change the mobile, and it's you Gautam who is going to note down as Sana's expenses".

Gautam agrees with a smile and reach out to the browsing center to book the ticket for Paul. All three are waiting for their turn in the browsing center.

News flashes in the TV in the browsing center, it is about a road accident near Mahabalipuram yesterday morning, it was about a Ferrari car crashed onto the divider and all three men inside the car died at the spot.

Sana and Gautam hear the news and rushes to watch the TV, they show all three dead men's photographs, Gautam sees Sana and she nods her head as yes.

Paul who is hazing the city outside the browsing center has no clue about this, but Sana and Gautam keenly watching the news channel.

The news also states "The all three men are drugged and the high dose of drug usage had led these men crash their car into the divider. The cops also seized three packages of aquatic cocaine bladders from the car that crashed, and they claim that, those aquatic cocaine bladders must be bought from Pondicherry."

Both Sana and Gautam looked at each other and said nothing and moved.

Another news flashes in the same channel, this time it is the news that shook Rameswaram, it is about Sana and her unattended bag.

News states "The unattended bag that was found on CMBT bus stand yesterday was claimed a young man as that belongs to his friend's sister, the cops enquired them they release the statement "The girl's family contacted us and they are on their way to collect the certificates and the bag." The SSLC certificate and the JEE hall ticket are in the name of Sana Amyra from Rameswaram is notable."

Both Sana and Gautam looked at each other again and stopped at the TV again.

Paul also joins them, now.

All three come out of the browsing center and looks at each other again.

Sana looks panicked, and says "So my family must be aware of where I must be, I don't know what happened to Latif, he must have been scared."

Gautam gasps and says "They must be aware now, but you need to grab your certificates back, then only you can purse your education."

Paul has no clue what they are talking about.

"Sana, its time, that we need to go to Chennai, no matter what" says Gautam.

Sana thinks for some time and says "No, my father must have sent people to Chennai, my life would end, if they find me there, and you know what? They said the family has contacted us, I think my father would have gone there as of now,". Sana cries and scares about her situation and firmly believes that her father would kill her.

"Uhhh, do you know your brother's phone number?" asks Gautam.

"No, I only remember my father's number, I have written somewhere in my notebook, but I lost it with my bag," said Sana.

Gautam wipes his face and says "Sana, we don't even a have a place to stay here."

Paul listening to both says immediately "Why don't you both come to Alister Wood Street, Glenmorgan."

Again, both Sana and Gautam looked at each other with shock, Sana stopped crying and looked at Paul with determination and Paul smiles.

CHAPTER NINETEEN

Gautam booked the tickets for Coimbatore in bus for all three, Paul, Sana, and himself.

Board the bus and it is semi sleeper multi axle bus, Paul and Sana again argues for window seat, but this time, Gautam asks both to sit in the window seat and he sits with Sana beside and leaves Paul with a stranger in the front seat.

Bus moves, Paul starts enjoying the window seat and Gautam tries to sleep. Sana looking and checking at Paul in regular interval, after sometime Paul starts missing Sana. He turned back towards Sana and Sana realizes that and she pretends to be sleeping, Paul feels so lonely again.

He wants Sana to be near him, and he needs her presence so he gets up and wakes up Gautam and asks him to sit in his seat, Gautam who is in half sleep agrees and Paul sits near to Sana finally and he realizes the real satisfaction of the journey.

Sana opened her eyes from the fake sleep and looks at Paul, both looking at each other and Paul slowly rest his head on Sana's shoulder.

As all three, Paul, Sana and Gautam are on their way to Glenmorgan, Latif reached Chennai and straight away goes to meet Sriram, and Sriram explained the critical situation at the police station.

Sriram says "They are suspecting me, as Sana's father refused to file a missing complaint, they feel I kidnaped her and I was playing with them".

"He won't be believing in law and orders, he always find his own way to solve problems, I feel, things are out of our hands now" says Latif.

"Latif, believe me I have a strong feeling that Sana will come back, she is somewhere near to us, she might have known the news and she will get back" Sriram consoles Latif and asked his friends to search Sana.

Latif prays at Sriram's house and literally breaks down to Sriram as her exam date was passed on yesterday. But Sriram confidently says "Leave the JEE exam, I believe Sana will get a seat in a reputed college in Tamil Nadu."

Meanwhile, Waqar's men from Keezhakarai and Ramnad district have rushed to Chennai to search Sana and they tactically surrounded the CMBT police station without fail. They also been informed by Waqar that they should not be involved in any legal activities and should not be open to anyone, if they opened the entire history of Sana being pregnant and her elope activity will come to limelight. They equally surrounded the police station and started keenly watching the station, they are waiting for Sana whom they think will come to collect the certificates and her bag.

But Sana was safely travelling to Glenmorgan with Paul and eventually Paul feels more safer on the shoulders of Sana.

They reached Coimbatore, near to Gandhipuram bus stand, Gautam buys a new mobile to insert Paul's sim as his old phone is not working. Sana also asks Gautam to note down his spendings again,

"In the name of Paul?" asks Gautam.

"No, continue in the name of Sana," said Sana.

Gautam squeezes lips and asks Paul to make a call and inform to your place. Suddenly Sana grabs the new cellphone and makes a call to Jacob through the number saved in the sim card.

Jacob answers in tension, who is in his middle of work at Dam's security office "Hey Paul, where are you?"

"No, it is Sana" replied Sana.

"What? What happened to Paul?" Jacob blabbered in tension as he was so tensed of Paul's cell phone being switched off for two days.

"He is here, we are in Coimbatore, we are coming" said Sana with excitement and gives the cell phone to Paul and asks him to speak.

"Hmm, I'm coming back, send our vehicle" says Paul over the phone.

"Welcome back, Paul," said Jacob.

All three boards the bus from Gandhipuram bus stand Coimbatore to Glenmorgan main village. In two hours, they reached Glenmorgan main village, they are received by Jacob and Henry.

Henry stares at Paul as he brings two new commers to the town and Paul asks Sana and Gautam to greet Henry, Both Sana and Gautam greet Henry but he delivers a fake smile deliberately.

They picked them up in a jeep and after a travel of thirty minutes they stopped at a place and Henry asks them to jump on a horse, the horse taxi service which is the only way to enter Glenmorgan valley. Sana hesitates for a horse ride as the horse-riding men are so new to her, Paul sees her and he immediately asks on horse rider to get down and he gets ready to ride the horse, Sana got excited and jumps onto the horse with Paul and he starts riding the horse, Gautam sees them with excitement and asks Henry to guide him to climb on the horse.

"Man, when did he learn horse riding?" Henry asks to Jacob.

"God knows the truth," said Jacob.

They enter the Glenmorgan Sir Alister Wood street, the street welcomes them with a wooden statue of Sir Alister Wood and Sana reads the inscriptions in it.

Several names in scripted on it namely Sir Alister Wood, Michael Raju, Alfred Mathew, Anna Catherine. After they reached the street, Mary comes out with her infant whose crying sound add more music alongside the beautiful weather of Glenmorgan.

The church at the Alister Wood street is so mesmerizing courtesy of the fog and snow aligned as a cover for the church tower and it slowly moves away in the way it unhides the tower. Gautam watches that church's gate is locked and he tries to ask about that to Jacob but Jacob curiously stares at Gautam which makes him uncomfortable.

Henry, Mary, and few other neighbors of them, all gathered to see both Sana and Gautam, Sana looks a bit uncomfortable as everyone looks at them both. Gautam manages to smile at everyone generously but somehow in a while he also lost his generosity. Slowly he asks Jacob about why everyone here is staring at them. Jacob did not answer but continued his stare.

Paul who did not considered anything calmy opens his house's door and immediately came out with a basket and starts asking every one's needs as a list to buy from main village up there near to dam.

Meanwhile, the church's father Louis come there by the cycle and opens the church and rings the bell. Father Louis also joins them in staring at both Sana and Gautam.

Jacob stops him and says "Paul, me and Henry have bought it yesterday, you please take rest and take care of your guests."

"Oh, yeah! I have brought guests from Pondicherry" said Paul and he asks Sana and Gautam to come in.

Sana enters the house, and Gautam sense that there is something mysterious in the way that everyone looks at them. He slowly enters the house by seeing everyone.

Paul's house excites both Sana and Gautam, the walls, that are filled with paintings in each corner. Only the fireplace is empty with no fire sticks and the chimney is not lightened up for some days since he left the home. Paul sees the very first painting, which started to fade away from the rain water is now completely faded. Paul keenly watches that place and gets traumatized suddenly and falls.

Sana and Gautam rescue him and calls Jacob and Henry.

After sometime Paul wakes up and scolds everyone neared to him,

"I said, I'm not a patient, I had Madeline to take care, but now I have got two new more guests to take care, don't treat me like a patient," says Paul.

Jacob stares at him and leaves the place without telling a word and Henry stares at both Sana and Gautam mysteriously.

Now Gautam also stares back at Henry and the stare game goes on for some minutes.

Sana urges Gautam to stop, he leaks tears as well but Henry has no idea to stop the game, as the game goes on, Paul slaps Henry to move away as he needs to go for his work. Paul tells Sana and Gautam to wait and have the fruits and cookies he made until he comes back from the valley.

Before that Paul reminds of the tomb in the backyard of his house and asks both Sana and Gautam to visit there, they both goes behind and a simple cross is place on the top of a mud filled area. Paul bends down and both Sana and Gautam follow him. They come back to house and Paul gets angry again to see Henry still being there, he slaps him in the head and says "Have you got the list?"

Henry again looks at both Sana and Gautam but leaves the house as Paul urged him to give the list. Paul leaves up to climb the mountain.

Dusk appears slowly in the west sky of Alister Wood street, Sana lies down in tired in the home watching the paintings of Madeline.

"Sana, I sense some mystery is hiding behind all these fog and snow" says Gautam.

"I guess, but I think Paul has nothing to do with, because he would have told us, right?" Sana replied.

"But what if the mystery lies within Paul?" asks Gautam. Sana replied nothing and looks at the painting in every corner and now every painting of Madeline looks mysterious to both. Gautam says "Let's find out".

Gautam asks Sana to stay here and he goes to James's tea shop, which is very few steps away from Paul's home. Gautam orders a ginger tea to Henry. Father Louis also comes there to eat cookies and ordered tea. Henry stares again towards Gautam and Gautam moved his eyes away and receives the tea. Gautam loves the tea very much and smiles at Father who sits straight in front of Gautam.

Gautam wants to know about the mysterious looking of everyone in the street to Father Louis, but Father also granted him the same mysterious look. Gautam gets up and leaves the place and walks to Paul's house and Sana comes out of the house in search of Gautam.

Both Henry and Father watches Gautam walking away, and Gautam asks Sana to go inside quickly, suddenly a woman voice calls "Sir" loudly, and Gautam turned towards the voice, it is Mary, wife of Henry. Henry immediately urges Mary to go inside and no to talk with him but Mary denies it and says "Enough is enough, we need to tell the truth, they both seems innocent".

Gautam and Sana look at each other and Gautam believe that the mystery is going to unfold.

Mary calls both inside their home and Henry follows them and he sees the two elephant's fighting drawing that was drawn by her father James and Paul many years ago.

"You please leave the place, as soon as possible, we feel this is not right you two being here for long" says Mary.

Gautam and Sana seem confused and looks at each other.

"We cannot get what are you talking about, we known Paul's entire story and how much he loved Madeline," says Sana, at the same time Gautam hold the hand of Sana and let Mary to talk.

Henry joins the conversation, "What we are saying is simple, have you seen Madeline?"

"No, we haven't," said Gautam.

"But she is dead, even before we meet Paul, how come we could have seen her" asks Sana.

"We are here since our birth; we didn't see Madeline either" says Henry and Mary.

Gautam and Sana are so confused and urged Mary and Henry to be clear.

"Madeline is not real, there is no one lived Madeline in this entire Alister Wood street, it is his hallucination, Madeline only lived in his painting, he consoled himself all these days that the Madeline, the best painting he made lived with him". Henry says with determined face.

Gautam and Sana stood shocked and they cannot believe what happened and how Paul has lived with a hallucinated character for all these years.

"But this could be not true, I have seen ear rings, the French warrior statue, everything and at last the tomb, whose tomb it is?" asks Sana with curiosity and seems tensed.

A cycle stops and a man from the cycle enters Henry's home, who is Jacob and Father Louis follows him up.

"Dear, we know, this must be shocking and unbelievable to know, but before coming to a conclusion you both need to know about Alister Wood Street and Paul, Paul Alfred Mathews" says Jacob.

CHAPTER TWENTY

As both Sana and Gautam freeze in shock, Jacob narrates the history of Paul and his family. He starts with the origin, Paul's father Alfred Mathew was Sri Lankan Tamil Christian belongs to Trincomalee, the place from the east coast of Sri Lanka. He was an orphan; he was brought up by a Portugal church's orphanage at Trincomalee. In the year, 1942, He moved to Uva province in his teenage to work in a tea estate at Nuwara Eliyah, the hill station. There he worked for almost ten years, in those years he spent time by plucking tea leaves and helping the church's father in Sunday masses.

In some time, one day when he was returning home from work, he saw a British girl is bullied by the fellow English school mates for not having blonde hair, as having blonde hair was stylish and seemed to be modern youths' trend in those days among English colonial places at that time, Young Alfred Mathew saw her and rescued her by saying, "People who have black hairs tends to be brainier because, more you use a product, the more it will get dark." After listening to him the young English girl started smiling and yelled back at her school mates and walked with Alfred Mathew, they got introduced after that and they used to follow the habit if walking together at that time regularly, they become good close friends, later Alfred came to know that she is Anna Catherine, the daughter of the Ceylon tea estate managing director, William Brooks. Both Anna Catherine and Alfred Mathew were in similar age group, so they find easy to get used to the habits and relationship.

Days and months later, their friendship turned into love. The love becomes forbidden at the very first moment they started loving as he was a Sri Lankan and she was a Britain.

They spent their love days and months in that estate's magical places and their love essence spread throughout the Nuwara Eliyah mountains. They used to see each other daily as Anna stands in the balcony in her house and Alfred walks down carrying the tea leaves bag on his shoulder.

Five year later in 1947, Anna's father William Brooks came to know about Anna and Alfred's love, so he decided to send back Anna to England to study. But she opposed and stayed strong in love relationship. But William Brook brought a man named Hooper Collins from England, a management studies scholar to marry Anna Catherine.

People working with Alfred Mathew opposed the decision of making Anna Catherine marry someone other than Alfred. Anna severely opposed marrying Hooper Collins but William was so adamant. The workers alongside Alfred protested against William in the estate but not cooperating with the estate's management and done a strike.

Alfred was so confident in saving Anna, but he eventually failed.

The estate management decided to sack everyone who protested against William so in order to save working people Alfred withdrew his love and decided to leave his Anna Catherine. He also apologized to the management but the management fired him. He lost job and become the horse rider with the help of his friend. He carried people and goods in between Nuwara Eliyah mountains.

In meantime, Anna Catherine got married with Hooper Collins

Few months later, when Alfred was riding horse, he was informed by his friend that Hooper Collins is flying back to England along with his relatives from India, as India is going to get independence from colonial British, they decided to leave early.

Immediately, he rushed to Anna's house and saw her standing alone in a balcony, where they used to see each other during their love days. Both saw each other again but with no real love moments.

Hooper Collins left Anna Catherine here as a symbol of divorcing her soon, as Anna was pregnant but they both never really involved in sex. Hooper Collins cursed Anna and William, then left Sri Lanka.

Anna Catherine, confessed to her father William that she was pregnant because of Alfred Mathew. William lost his cool and slapped her daughter but later Alfred Mathew rescued her and took her away from her house. William legally part ways with her daughter due to her act.

In few months, the baby boy was born and they named him Paul. The couple built a small shelter house inside the estate's premises. Few months later, Sri Lanka got independence and the small estate was taken over by Sri Lankan government. They decided to close the small revenue estates, which includes William Brook's estate too. So, the Brook's family decided to leave England.

Every property was taken over by the landlords of Sri Lanka and so many workers lost their job and left stranded. Alfred and Anna decided to go to India with their infant, Paul. So, they decided to leave to India for work.

They board the boat mail and reached Dhanushkodi, they were mesmerized by the beauty and the activities of one of the top busiest cities of India at that time. They roamed around everywhere and they could not find a job for them. Finally, they meet a man at Post office who sends letter to his family. They came to know that he is Michael Raju, from Glenmorgan, Ooty hills. He was working as a track man in the railways department in Dhanushkodi. After talking for some time, Michael came to know that they both worked in tea estate and reminds about the tea estate back in his home village Glenmorgan.

He promised that he would get them there, and as promised, in a week they went to Glenmorgan.

Alfred and Anna entered Glenmorgan valley and admired by the beautiful weather along with the tea estate, which was ran by a former British officer Alister Wood, he decided to stay back with people of Glenmorgan lower valley even after the independence, but still he gave the entire estate to the people of the village and asked them to manage by themselves, the concept of no owner, no managers liked by both Alfred and Catherine. Alister Wood just understood that the people of lower place find everything so hard even for the essentials, so he decided to plant a very small tea estate and initiated a small trade from them, he invested everything from his own pocket. The valley has two residential areas one is main village, another one is valley down there. It has only four streets. The four streets are named after St. John's, St. Peter's, St. Xavier, St. Romario.

Alfred Mathew and Michael Raju become good friends. Michael Raju has a wife named Esther and two kids, one daughter named Isabella and a son named James.

Plantations and the cultivation techniques of Alfred and Anna were so new to the people of Glenmorgan and eventually it yielded good results. The trade becomes better. Alister Wood was so impressed by the management of both Alfred and Anna

A year passes by, it was Christmas 1949, it was raining heavily, Alister wood organized a Christmas party in the streets of lower part of Glenmorgan. Everyone gathered at church including, Alfred, Anna, Paul, Michael Raju, Esther, Isabella, and James. In between the party, Alister Wood was talking to everyone at the street, he finds that Michael Raju is the only man from the street who works away from the place, so he asked him to switch his place and start working here, Michael Raju also realized and said that he is also in an idea of starting a tea stall business in the street, to produce tea fresh from our estate. Alister Wood appreciated him.

Then, Alister Wood meets a new comer and he was the new trader for the tea leaves, the new company from England which was dealt by Alister Wood himself by marketing as the original Ceylon tea with much lesser whole sale price made in India. The English company got impressed and sent their managing director Glenmorgan, it was whom Alister Wood is talking to.

Both Alfred and Anna shocked to see the new comer as it is Hooper Collins.

After dealing with Alister Wood, Collins also shocked to see both Anna and Alfred here. At the church, Collins meets Anna and spoke few words. Collins showed interest on Anna again and he confessed that he wants to be with Anna.

"I missed your beauty," said Collins. Anna got tensed and searches for Alfred who was busy distributing the sweets. Collins held the hands of Anna firmly and Anna resists from him. Suddenly he called Alfred and Alfred immediately saw this happening and ran towards them.

Suddenly, that place starts to shake heavily.

A huge part of land, slides from the top of mountain, suddenly everyone rushing back to their huts and Alister Wood calls his workers stay inside the house. Due to the heavy eruption, everything in the streets smashed away, Anna firmly held her son Paul and stuck in between two rocks. Due to the heavy slides, the rock that Anna was stuck got deviated and washed away down with the help of rain water.

Alister Wood saw her and immediately caught the little Paul in his hands and asks for help, Alfred who is saving Collins from a cliff, Collins begs for his life and Alfred saves him, he then rushed back to Alister Wood and he is standing with Paul in his hand and the rock that Anna stuck gets rolled down deeper into the valley. Alfred did not see Anna rolling but he saw a black colored hair that stuck between rock rolling over and deeper he hears a scream from Anna, Alfred screams back heavily and he didn't believe that Anna was gone.

"I didn't see her falling, she must be here," said Alfred. Alister Wood cries and breaks down in tears. Alfred turns and see Collins standing and he starts cursing him that he took her away to England. Heavy traumatization hits Alfred instantly and he starts chasing Collins which made Collins fell and got washed away by mud. He then searches for his wife.

Alister Wood saw him acting vigorously, locked him in his room and rescued people one by one with the help of his worker. Michael lost her daughter Isabella and he seen crying. Alister Wood locked few people in his house which was built in the way to escape landslides. He almost saved the half of the population by rescuing them single handedly.

Rain stops slowly and he saw the church is hanging and the Jesus statue is left alone and it is almost at the cliff and about to fall. Alister Wood went to the church and pulled up the Jesus statue and suddenly a rock flew and hits Alister Wood and he fell off from the cliff along with the Jesus statue. The entire street saw Alister Wood, the Messiah of them falling along with Jesus' statue and they left helpless as the man who gave everything until his last breath has died.

The rainwater drained, the lands aligned, the houses were re built but the pain it left has not. The people re named the street to Alister Wood.

Alfred left with his son, still never got out of Traumatization searches for Anna and sometimes even shouts Collins's name. Sometimes he even tried to go down in the valley to search Anna.

Years passed, People slowly getting back to cultivation and tea trade that was marketed by Alister Wood which still helps for the people of this place, Paul was slowly growing up, he made friends with James, son of Michael Raju.

People of Alister Wood street raised a wooden statue made by them and place at the entrance of the street. They also in scripted the names of whom contributed to it.

Few years later one day, when Paul was five-year-old, he and James climbed up above the valley to play. They saw an elephant family there, both Paul and James got panicked and ran away but they saw from a certain distance. As they were watching two elephants, a mother elephant and its calf were standing near a tree, suddenly a branch from a tree broke and fell off and it was about to hit the elephant calf, suddenly the mother elephant grabbed the broken branch from its tusk and saved her calf.

"That's how a mother reacts to save her kid," said James.

Paul thought about her mother and returned home, he went to his father and asked said about the elephant incident to his father. He also asked about his mother and Alfred had got no clue about what to answer.

Alfred got emotional and hugged his son, and told "You do not have to be worried; you know where you mother went? She had gone to meet her parents in England, she will get back one day and you should be a proud son for her."

"How did she go from here, daddy?" asked Paul.

"She flew with the wings like an angel from the cliff, and she will come back," said Alfred.

Paul completely believed what his father said he made the habit of watching the valley down there, he also imagined himself that how his mother would have flown with her wings from the cliff. He then started waiting for her mother to comeback from the valley by flying with her wings.

At that time, Michael Raju also built a new house in such way that it is completely safe from the erosion. Paul sees the newly built clay house wall and it he predicted that it was apt to draw something as he is fond of drawing.

He drew a scene that he saw above, that of a lovable moment between a mother elephant and her calf. Alfred finds it started scolding him but Michael Raju's family appreciated it.

Alfred got saddened about the memories of Anna and disturbed by the activities of Paul, who longs for his mother's love. He got traumatized more. One day at night, he saw Paul was missing from his bed and he went out to search him and finally found him at the cliff, Paul sitting alone biting his nails heavily and was keenly watching down the valley. Alfred nudged him and asked him, "What are you watching?"

"I'm waiting for my mom to come, daddy," said little Paul. Alfred got emotional again and as he was already traumatized, he said to his son that he would go down and get her mother. He also promised that he would get his mother back.

Next day morning, the entire Alister Wood street was so tensed and every one was in hurry of searching Alfred. Paul woke up from his sleep to see Michael Raju crying and Paul came to know that his father is missing. As per as the promise, Alfred went down the valley to get Anna back but he himself never got back.

Entire Alister Wood street is saddened by this and Paul left alone in his life, he was also taken care by the people of that street. As years passed by, Paul began to work for tea estate following the foot prints of his parents. He also involved in trading. In few years due to another landslide, the predominant path to reach Alister Wood street is completely made unusable and the street lost the complete communication with the main village. People of that street also petitioned several government and non-governmental agencies but every one they approached least cared about this street, as they are very much less in numbers, but their tea trade never stopped.

Meanwhile, Paul grown up and he learned to read and write at the church. They teach kids of the street as they find difficult to reach the school from there. Meanwhile in 1964, Michael Raju lost his life in a heavy cyclone that wiped out entire Dhanushkodi, while he was working at railway track in a heavy rain, he was hit by a huge wave prior to another major accident of a passenger train. So, James and his family started the own business which was the idea of his father. Due to that, James needed more raw materials to cook and they are in also in need of milk.

The nearest cattle farm in up above the valley, near to the dam. But the regular pathway to connect is closed and became un usable, so they are finding it hard to get the stuffs from there. So, Paul appointed himself to serve the street, he decided to climb up above the valley to reach the Glenmorgan reservoir dam area and find the essential raw materials. This has become Paul's regular job as everyone will give a certain amount of money as a share from the tea trade to Paul and for the voluntary work he does.

The loneliness has filled Paul's life. To overcome that, he skilled himself in painting, he started painting the scenes he saw and he drew illustrations from the stories he heard. He also illustrated many biblical scenarios. Among them, the best he drew was the art of Holy Mother Mary and Jesus Christ, which got selected for the art exhibition 1971 in Pondicherry, where he met Madeline.

"Madeline?" asks Sana to Henry.

"Yeah, it was true that both my father James and Paul met Madeline at Pondicherry back in 1971, but things didn't happen in a way that Paul must have narrated his story to you" says Henry.

Sana looks confused and she tries to explain every place she went with him Pondicherry.

"My father told me, Paul met Madeline Ivy an Indo France drawing teacher worked in a school managed by French government, they talked for hours under the French warrior statue, Paul in fact asked Madeline to meet again at the rock beach in that evening, both my father and Paul also waited for some time at the beach along with the ear ring he bought for her but Madeline didn't turn up to meet him" says Henry.

Both Sana and Gautam listening to him keenly.

Henry continued "Paul was so upset as he believed that Madeline would come and meet him again, my father insisted him to go to her school and check again, so they went and asked about Madeline at the French school, there her colleague gave one letter to Paul which Madeline gave her to give to Paul."

"What was written in the letter, do you have that?" asks Sana. Henry asks everyone to come to Paul's house and takes out the bag from the loft near the fire place. It contains some paintings and a box, he opened the box and shows the old ear ring he bought for her in Pondicherry back in 1971 and it has a letter folded, Henry reads in front of everyone.

"Dear Artist, I'm so glad that I met you, I know you would come and search me that is why I'm reaching out to you through this, by the time you are reading this letter, I would have left this beautiful place, I was called by my uncle to come back home already, I was ready to leave this place freely as I have no one here to tell as a relative except the sea, all these days I was preparing myself to leave from here. Yesterday was my last day at Pondicherry, but both fortunately or unfortunately I met you, I can sense how we both felt after talking for few hours under Bertrand du Guesclin statue, I bet you still cannot get the exact pronunciation of that but hope one day you will. It was like a dream and in those hours, I felt like talking to myself, in fact the better version of me, that is you. Please paint more and I hope the holy love keeps showering on you all day – Madeline Ivy".

Henry closed the letter and both Sana and Gautam standing in shock and they could not believe this. Henry also mentioned that his father told everything to him before his death due to pneumonia in 2001.

"Then Paul came back here, but he never really got over his loneliness, he used to read this letter often in regular period of time and gets depressed. He then drew this painting of Madeline from his heart, the very first one and he started living with this painting he imagined stuffs, he used to tell my father that Madeline was at home, my father believed and went to his house to see there is no one except the wall full of paintings of Madeline, at that point James realised that Paul hallucinates as Madeline lives with him. He in fact cooked pan cakes for her, sometimes he used to bake cakes but he forgets about that and goes up for his work by keeping the pan switched on, so many times me and Mary rushed into his house and switched off the stove with heavily roasted pan cakes. But the interesting part is the next day Paul used to tell me that Madeline has fought with me so she has given him the roasted pan cakes, he also used to buy more carrots saying that for Madeline, but I have seen him eating it alone, he used to sleep right under the very first painting of Madeline, which is now faded away by the rain drops."

Sana starts to cry slowly and Gautam realises that how deep and strong a man longed for a love, a care, a companion to be with, Gautam also able to realise about the mental distraction and the trauma that Paul must have got is un real. He also watches the old painting of Madeline get faded away and he glanced at every painting.

Jacob consoles Sana and says "You both are the ones whom now Paul loves, but you both must have separate lives to live, you cannot be here, so another loss of his loved one puts him in the trauma that could well end up in ending him."

Gautam asks about the tomb in the backyard, Father Louis explains that it was nothing but a drama by Henry to make sure that Paul believes that Madeline does not exist anymore.

"But he becomes more depressed after that, that is why me and Uncle Jacob planned to send him to Pondicherry we believed the place where it all began will put an end to it, but the mysterious thing we all couldn't figure out is that how Madeline died within his hallucination" says Henry.

"The painting" replies Gautam. Everyone looked at him.

"Ever since the painting started fading away, Paul thought himself that Madeline is getting sick and eventually she started fading away from his mind, see hallucination is simple it is more often comes from adaptations, Paul adapts the painting as his wife, so once the rain water completely faded away the painting, Paul hallucinated that Madeline is dead" says Gautam, and everyone seems believing him.

Father Louis says "Praise the Lord."

Suddenly Paul enters the house, "Is everyone here?" asks Paul. He gave the milk can to Henry and taps on the shoulders of Jacob and says "Man, I was searching for you up there, but you are here" then he got blessings from Father and gave the carrots he got to both Sana and Gautam and asks them to eat and says "Just wait for some time, I'll make fresh pan cakes for you both." Paul goes to the kitchen and everyone leaves the house.

Both Sana and Gautam holding the bunch of carrots and looking at each other.

CHAPTER TWENTY-ONE

That night, after Paul fell asleep both Sana and Gautam are sitting outside the house with the separate woolen blankets over them. Both are still in shock and they are unable to digest the fact that his love towards Madeline is out of complete hallucination.

"Loved and to be loved is the basic thing that one needs in life, but this hadn't got neither thing" Gautam says and looks at Sana who looks back at him and agrees with him through her eyes.

"It shouldn't have been that easy for him to realize that his love of life isn't real" Sana says in a low voice.

"But his love is real" Gautam replied.

Both stars looking above and the snow filled sky slowly opens to show them the cluster of stars which all over the sky.

Sana says by looking up to the stars "Love is precious, loving people shouldn't be subjective, I have a question to our system where we live, why we people are always supposed to love someone for something, like for lust, for commitment, for ecstasy, for cuddles, for happiness, but what Mr. Grandpa gained by his love is nothing, what he received back is totally nothing...nothing but love, that un explainable feeling that made the world a better place to live, not only an ample atmosphere that left us to live here, there is also a thing called love".

Gautam looking at Sana with admiration as a seventeen-year-old girl explains about love of the world, he smiles and says "As per as your concept, Love and being loved wins the battle with survival of the fittest theory, what do you think? Which made the world in between the two theories."

"Can you explain what is survival of the fittest?" asks Sana.

Gautam thinks for a while and replies, "Uhh, I'll tell you an example, a dense forest caught fire and only four animals left in the entire forest a cow, a lion, a tiger and a fox, all four are in heavy hunger, first cow searched for a some plans or grass to eat, then lion and tiger searched for some animals to eat, then came the fox who found the cow using the earth's magnetic field, the only animal which has such significance to stalk its prey for you know usually fox don't hunt for food especially the cow, which it cannot as the cow can easily smash fox, so the fox made a strategy, it found that the both lion and tiger are searching for food and the only food left is this cow, so it informed about the cow to both the animals s both goes to the same place to hunt the cow, first lion attacked cow, then tiger attacked the cow, the cow injured and fell down but in extreme hungriness, both lion and tiger fought for the cow's meat which lead to the biggest fight between two animals, as a result both animals killed each other and both lion and tiger fell dead, then the fox arrived and happily ate the entire beef meal that day, so who survived now? Which is the fittest animal?"

"The Cow" replies Sana.

Gautam looks confused, "No, it is the fox, it actually killed all three animals."

"But cow never thought about killing the lion or tiger or the fox, right?" asks Sana. Gautam sighs and turned up.

"Sana, survival of the fittest is subjective" says Gautam.

"But love isn't subjective, it is eternal, it lasts long" says Sana.

"Nothing wins here Sana, the world is made of blending both love and being loved then survival of fittest, we cannot change it overnight and we just have to be a survivor of love," says Gautam

Sana blinks and says "Humans are dangerous, they do both, that is why I fear of people, I even don't know how I am as a human, I don't know what I chose"

Gautam inhales and says "In April 1889, two kids were born in Europe in different places, both brought up in a very poor financial background, both brought up in an unhealthy family setup but later in their lives, one chose to make people happy and the other one chose to kill people, their names were Charlie Chaplin and Adolf Hitler, it is up to you, whom do you want to be".

As Gautam says this, the fog eventually closes the sky again.

The next morning when Henry wakes up opens the shop, he finds lights is switched on inside Paul's house, he goes to Paul's house and enters inside. He sees Paul has been searching for something behind the paintings and the paint box, Henry asks "What are you searching for?"

"I have seen Gautam and Sana here, now they are missing" says Paul.

Both Sana and Gautam seem walking on the un finished roads from where they came through by the horse. They also carry their bags, they hire the jeep and goes to Ooty, from there they plan to go to Chennai.

Henry informs Mary about Gautam and Sana left the street and they seem pretty happy that Paul will not be depending on something here after and he might not be missing them. He also informs Father Louis about this and he instantly rushes onto Paul's house and he sprays the holy water throughout his houses and says "Praise the Lord."

That day, when Paul went up above the valley and he meets Jacob at reservoir dam and says "Gautam and Sana have left the place, seems like they have their own lives". Jacob smiles and he is happy that Paul realizes the reality of losing something and he says "Paul, that's okay, lets love what you love the most, the street, Sir Alister Wood street."

Paul smiles back and leaves.

Next day, midnight 8 PM, Gautam and Sana reach Chennai CMBT, they go to the police station and Sana collects her bag and certificates. Waqar's men who were waiting around the police station is not aware of Sana walks in but one man who is in half sleep slightly identifies her and wakes up.

The cop from the police station informs, that this place was surrounded by her father's men and they were waiting for her to catch her.

"We cannot understand your father, he didn't file a complaint, please be safe the morons outside looking terrifying and us, the cops even cannot question them as the major consequences would arise," says the cop.

Gautam asks Sana no to worry and says "I'm here, nothing happens."

By the time, they are talking inside the station, the men have surrounded outside the police station, Sana looks worried and Gautam gets up to see them.

Inside police station, there are two female sex workers, who were arrested by the cops for doing brothel inside the bus stand, both listened the entire conversation between Sana, Gautam and the cop comes up to them and says "Kid, don't worry we take care of you."

"Hey, get away" says the cop.

"Sir, believe us we will get back" says a sex worker and takes both Sana and Gautam out of the station. The men outside started nearing Sana and a sex worker immediately whistles and numerous women gathered near to them whom are all sex workers. They begin to beat them, thinking that they involved in harassing the sex worker who whistled, as that was the signal used for safety purpose when some morons misbehave with them.

As they are beating and threatens them, these two sex workers call their friend who drives the auto and asks him to take them out of here.

They kiss Sana on their forehead and says "Study well, a woman's education will save an entire generation." Sana earns the immense warmth with that kiss then smiles and both Sana and Gautam get into auto.

Immediately both the sex workers, walk back into the police station calmly.

Gautam asks the auto driver to leave them in a hotel, they go to the hotel at Vada Palani and finished the dinner. Gautam pays the bill.

"Please note it down the spendings, it is getting more and more" says Sana.

"It won't be getting much more" Gautam replies with a smile.

"I don't feel that I will be getting back to Rameswaram, I feel scared, for the first time I have seen this world" Sana says and looks at Gautam.

"And it has more people than molecules and atoms" Sana says and looks away from Gautam.

"Please don't be worried about your future, we will look for another chance, entrance exams are not the only way to be graduate, that shouldn't be fair too, you have invested all these years in learning and getting passed in a reputed exam not clearing entrance wouldn't be a barrier for your twelve years of learning, we will get through proper counselling for Engineering," Gautam says and motivates Sana and promises her to keep her safe with him.

Gautam asks about Sriram's address and Sana searches for it, she finally finds it in a note, written by Latif. They both reaches to Sriram's house through auto from Vada Palani to Saida pet and knocked the door, whose house is in the first floor.

Sriram opens it, sees Gautam, and asks "Yeah, what can I do for you?"

Latif sees Gautam and then Sana sees Latif, suddenly Sana runs towards Latif and hugs him. Latif realizes it is Sana and he emotionally breaks down in tears.

"Alhamdulillah..." says Latif. Gautam smiles and Sana smiles back at him. Sana starts saying about Gautam,

"This is Gautam, and in one line, Sana wouldn't have been alive if there is no Gautam", says Sana.

Gautam sighs and smiles again and says "Gautam wouldn't have been smiling without Sana". Latif and Sriram looking at each other and suddenly a car arrived at their gate, Sriram go to see them, that is Waqar and his men.

Sriram turned around and says "It's your father."

Sana loses her cool and seem so scare, Latif pulled her under the sofa and asks Gautam to stay behind the kitchen wall.

Waqar rushes into the house, immediately Sriram tries to call his friends but Waqar stopped him.

"Latif, I failed" says Waqar. Latif shocks to hear Waqar.

"I failed as true Muslim, I put something on the same scale of Allah, I failed as father whom lost the daughter to the evil society, I failed as a human, I have made decisions for the society and community but not for my daughter, I blindly believed that only my daughter has committed the mistake but I completely faded out how the cruel world has ditched her" says Waqar.

Latif says "It is too late to confess; Allah won't be forgiving you."

"I know, let me deal that in after life, but I believe that my daughter will forgive me in my actual life" says Waqar.

Latif says in anger tone, "This is also too late, where is Sana? Where would you search your shining star?"

Waqar immediately shouts at Latif, "Hey...enough of drama, I can easily sense my daughter's presence, ask her to come out."

Latif and Sriram looking at each other and men around them look clueless.

"Sana, I have seen you, enough of drama and come out" shouts Waqar. Meanwhile, Gautam tried to come out of kitchen but Latif signaled not to come as Waqar is furious. Sana slowly comes out from the sofa and stands up.

Waqar looks at Sana and asks "Where is your hijab?"

Sana replied nothing.

"Where is your hijab?" Waqar asks again with a raising voice.

Sana replied nothing again.

"Where is your hijab?" Waqar asks furiously.

"Wappa, Chennai is much hotter and this is April month, I felt so hot, I would have ended up being Sana'wich by this heat, that's why I didn't need it now" says Sana.

"Okay, let's wait for the winter" Waqar says with a normal voice.

"Then, we will be having scarfs" Sana says and looks at Latif.

"But hijab is quite cheaper than expensive scarfs," Waqar says politely.

“Oh, if so, I choose hijab” Sana says and smiles.

“Everything is fine, but due to all your acts, she missed her JEE” says Latif.

“I know she missed that, but doors aren’t closed for her Engineering, I have bought application from Anna University, she might get placed on the basis of counselling ranking,” says Waqar.

Everyone shocks, and Sana cannot believe what her father has done and she starts being emotional, meanwhile from behind the kitchen wall, Gautam also surprised about Waqar’s act.

“But before that Sana must be clear of what her future is, I mean what is up with the thing she is carrying?” asks Waqar.

“I carry nothing, I carry nothing right from my baby to guilt, the evil society has given me that “thing” according to Wappa...” says Sana and Waqar interrupts in the middle, “See, I didn’t mean in that way...”

“No Wappa, there is no need of mentions here after, Allah has given me through the society, and Allah has taken it away from me through with the same society, Alhamdulillah!” says Sana and she smiles with pain.

Waqar realizes that she is aborted tears fed up in eyes and he comes closer to his daughter, he touches her abdomen and literally crises and he hugs her completely and his tears has made his bear wet. Sana also breaks down and she cries loudly.

Latif watches it and he also cannot control his emotion, Waqar apologized towards Latif and Latif stops him and he hugged them, all three Waqar, Sana and Latif are hugging together and Gautam looks at them and realizes that he is no longer needed for Sana.

Then, Waqar thanks Sriram and he also denies and says "Uncle, you are a brave man". Waqar shakes his head and says "I'm a father of a brave girl."

Sana blinks her eyes and looks at Waqar's face.

"Come on, let's go to our place and do the rest" says Waqar and Latif smiles and wipes his tears, then he taps at Sana's shoulders and pinches her cheeks.

Sana's face slowly fades down, she turns back and sees towards kitchen and Gautam showed his hand and symbolically says with his hands to "go."

Sana looks at Latif and he shakes his head and asks Sana to go.

Waqar, Latif and Sana leaves Sriram's house and gets into the car. Car starts, Sana puts her head out of window and looks up towards Sriram's house and he cannot find Gautam watching at them, but he is right up there hiding behind a curtain and watches Sana's car goes by with a heavy heart. Gautam then realizes that he is going to miss Sana more than he expected.

He started to feel her absence right from very first second, she left him.

Sana keeps on thinking about Gautam in the car, and Gautam keeps on thinking about Sana in the bus on his way to his house at OMR.

Gautam reaches the house, he opens the door, switches on light.

He hazes the laptop, the cellphone, the TV, the speakers, empty beer bottle, unwashed cloths, formal shoes, perfume bottle and his ID card. He gasps and he listens to the traffic sound, the office sound, computer keyboard typing sound, mouse clicking sound, tea stall sound, cigarette lighting sound, bottle opening sound, lift closing sound.

He closes his ears and stops illusioned sounds to his ears and falls in the couch.

CHAPTER TWENTY-TWO

Six months later...the same room in OMR, Gautam still lives alone and he comes out from the bathroom. He wipes his head and eats breakfast. His hall set up is now completely new and it is filled with travel bags, trekking shoes, high-definition cameras. A new go pro camera is placed on his table.

He calls to his parents on a conference call as usual, and he placed the phone on the table and he is busy wearing the socks.

"Again, I'm saying, I don't like your new job, its completely meaningless, I mean what is the point in roaming around places and recording it, how many watch that with interest?" says his mother over the phone.

His father interrupted and says "I wish you should have continued your previous job that's where you were paid better, and I feel this is completely unsafe, you go to places and meet someone new, I mean how come you know that they are good people?"

"Yes, this is will not suit you Gautam, I agree with your father, please understand, you are not a kid to keep yourself busy in things you love, you are an adult, you are at a stage where you should be pleasing the society" his mom advises him.

"Yeah, you are right, see your mom is right! Why you just cannot listen to us?" says his father.

Gautam takes the phone and answers "For the first time in all my twenty-five years, I have seen my mom and father stands at same point, but that shouldn't affect me either, Mom, yeah people don't watch these with interest but things will become vital in evolution, in some years, my videos on YouTube will be watched by millions, and Dad, believe me, this will earn me money the internet evolution will do it nicely, didn't your finance company predict it?".

His parents stay silent over the phone, "Dear Mom and Dad, I love what I do, see I love meeting new people, nothing excites me more than that, I'll never fail to make you proud or at least I will never let you down in any situation in life, Love you both."

Gautam cuts the call and sees mirror, gets ready and calls Lurdhu,

"Hello Gautam..." says Lurdhu over the phone.

"Anna, how are you?" asks Gautam, "Yeah, I am fine here, how is your new job, what did you? Is it vulgar or something?" says Lurdhu.

"Anna, that is vlogger" Gautam replies with a smile, "Yeah, that is" Lurdhu smiles too.

"How is Rani sister? Errr, she is my sister-in-law now, right?" asks Gautam. Lurdhu blushes over phone and Gautam teases him for the blush and says "Happy for you anna"

Lurdhu been silent for few seconds and says "Nothing is possible without Lord. Gautam"

"Happily, the peaceful live, discarding both victory and defeat, said by real Lord. Gautam Buddha" says Gautam.

"Yeah Gautam, I have got a ride to go, will call you back," says Lurdhu and he now owns an auto rikshaw and he rides around Chennai.

Gautam then starts his bike and goes to Adayar, he waits at a signal and checks the time and it is 01.15 PM. He then seems to be so hurried and ready for the signal to turn green. When the green signal comes, he rushes his bike to a tea shop at Adayar and parks the bike and starts looking around checked the time is now 01.30 PM. He gasps and suddenly he has been hit on the head from the back, that is Sana who carries a bag in her shoulder, a question paper and a scale in her.

Sana joined at Anna University to pursue an engineering degree in Information Technology which her father bought the application for, she had enough of cut off marks in her HSC exams. She had just finished the semester practical exams and now ready to join Gautam for three days, after she plans to go home and use the study holidays form first semester.

"I have been waiting here for ten minutes, where you have been" asks Sana.

"As usual, stuck in traffic" Gautam replies.

"Fraud, I know you must have got up from the bet at 12.30, cheater" Sana says in anger, and Gautam murmurs "I shouldn't have found you again with the help of your brother..."

"Come again?" says Sana and starts beating him heavily with the scale she had in her hands.

Gautam resists and says "Hey hey hey Sana, look...I have bought the tickets, we are going to Glenmorgan."

Sana stops beating and looks at him with a warm face, Gautam signals her to get on the bike and both goes to eat Biryani.

As they eat Biriyani, Sana delivers the usual dialogue "Keep everything noted, one day I'll become a CEO of an IT company and will pay your bills back." Gautam nods his head and does not care about her.

Sana opens the voice message from her father "Alhamdulillah, hope you finished your exams well, when are you coming?"

Sana replies through voice message as well, "In two three days Wappa, we are going to Glenmorgan, I told you about a grandpa, right? and Gautam is with me, we will be back in three days."

Gautam shouts "Insha'Allah" at Sana's phone and sends it.

That night, they board the bus and reaches Ooty next morning, as usual they hire the jeep from Ooty and reached Glenmorgan main village through the jeep and waits for Henry to come with horse. After sometime, Henry arrives and he collects the bag from Gautam and all three, Henry, Gautam and Sana enter Sir Alister Wood street in the morning.

They see every place with fond of great memories they had from the very little stay, Henry's son has grown a bit now. He can walk now and they named him John.

Mary opens Paul's house and asks them to wait there as Paul has gone up there for his morning duty. Both Sana and Gautam hazes around the house and they find the old Madeline's paintings are slightly faded but they find a new painting is covered by a cloth at the place where the very first Madeline's painting was there and it got vanished completely few months ago. Both Sana and Gautam look at each other and Sana slowly removes the cloth and they both shocks.

Paul has painted both Sana and Gautam at that place, both gets emotional and the door opens. Paul enters the house with bunch of carrots and calmly says "Oh, hello! Where you both have been? Safely back?"

Both Sana and Gautam rushes onto Paul and hugs him tightly and Paul eases their shoulders and says "Shall we have some pan cakes together?"

Paul makes the pan cakes and he brings three plates, and all three eat together near the fire place.

A slight drizzle arrives, Paul feels wholesome as finally he eats pancakes in real with the ones he loves so much and he realizes that the people in real are also more lovable, not only in paintings. Drizzle starts to be raining, the few rain water drops splashed into the floor and some hit both Sana and Gautam.

Instantly Paul reacts to it and catches some rain droplets and says "I won't let you two too to get faded away." Sana and Gautam smiles.

After the rain ends, Paul takes them to the small tea estate and shows them about the cultivation. Paul starts playing with Sana in the estate. In meantime, Gautam caught the entire street and spoke about it in the video, he then finally opens the camera and records again.

He opens the camera and says "Hey guys, this is Gautam again from Sir Alister Wood street, Glenmorgan as we seen, this place lacks improvement, they have petitioned several governments and also NGOs, many are interested in this place to acquire, but not to develop, people here never really connected with the outer world completely, especially the medical emergencies, recently a woman named Mary gave birth to her son through the horse, and also education, there is no easy access to education here, they need to be taken care and finally the man, the milkman of Sir Alister Wood street, without him this street wouldn't have survived all these years, and meet Mr. Paul Alfred Mathew son of Mr. Alfred Mathew and Anna Catherine who were the main architect of a small tea estate here,

which you see now".

Paul feels surprised and excited about Gautam telling his parents name and he the smiles at him, Gautam smiles back and Sana joins them.

Gautam says in the camera "and that's it, thank you so much everyone for watching this journey, hope you enjoyed a lot and we will be back soon with another great journey with experience until then its Paul – Sana and Gautam, do like share and subscribe, Tata."

Gautam calls both Paul and Sana to stand together and ready to click a selfie, and he tells both "Smile please." Sana smiles with ease and Paul delivers his trademark innocent smile. Gautam clicks the selfie of smile and from that moment they start believing that the best ingredient of life is smile.

Acknowledgements

Firstly, I thank you for reading this book. Now I have a huge list of names whom I would like to express my gratitude.

My mom, V. Thamil, who is being my everything, she is a pillar of my strength who shaped me with courage and love. Thanks for letting me know who I am and what I can do. It is my mom's influence which made me a writer, thanks for feeding me the habit of reading and writing to me. You are an engineer by profession, writer by passion and you are my first inspiration.

My dad, K. Subramanian, I hope the beautiful soul of yours loves me along with the universe. You always wanted me to do something and achieve my dreams. I miss your advice and suggestions to this book and I miss, you reading this book, I miss showing this to you, I miss making you proud but I am sure that you would have liked the first work of your son. Miss you dad.

My grandfather, K. Veerasamy, the icon of our family's literacy. The courage, confidence, and the energy you given to us in your time drives us to go places and achieves what we thrive for. No one could fill the void that you left. Thank you for the teachings Thatha, I will try to carry out your legacy forward with the blessings of your beautiful soul.

I would like to thank all my school teachers for making me who I am now, right from my kinder garden to twelfth grade. I feel, I was blessed to have such teachers, without them no one can pass through life with a moral. Next, I thank my college professors, who had the complete faith in me, been jovial and encouraged me throughout.

Friends are more like a family, being not only a companion also as a strength and energy.

Meenu, who stood beside me in all my ups and downs, sharing the knowledge and care together. You have been with me throughout this entire process and journey, keeping the faith in me. Thanks for being my support system.

Sowndharya, the one who always cares and checks me regularly, no matter where I am and what I do. Thanks for being there and spraying out the drops of motivation and courage since childhood.

Harsha, she is the first reader of my world. Without you, this would not have been possible. You have taken the special care of this novel more than me; without your inputs and suggestions I would have stuck somewhere in between the process. You believed that I could do this more than me. Thanks for being a guiding light.

Raghuveer anna, the mentors never say they are, they just provide you the tips and strategy constantly. What I am today is what he made me in last two years. Undoubtedly the go to person for everything I go through, the one initiated this process and gave me the confidence that I can achieve this.

Jacqueline, she is one of few who makes me feel that I can do something. Her energy is contagious, and the areas we covered in our discussions helped me to attain better understandings and thank you for the foreword.

Ramiyan, we all have that one person with us whom we travel decades together. Yor are the first person I annoyed by narrating stories. Vidhyadharan, for helping me in structure of characters and exploring places. The one who taught me that exploring a new place is the best feeling ever.

Rasim, that one person who understands everything even without I wanted to explain it. No one knows my ideology and thought process better than him. Thanks for listening to my blabbering of thoughts. Anbu Ramji, some days would not have been passed better without him. One who stood with me when I was down. Thank you for saving me from drowning into depression and kept me focused on writing process.

Wara, the one whom I can chip in to discuss any topic in the world. Our general discussions have helped me to become a better writer. Dr. Raja Pradeep, someone who shares enormous knowledge and think tank, thanks for being with me all these years. Keerthi Vassan, who almost listened my half-cooked stories in my college days and thanks for lending your ears.

Rathnakumar Raghunath, brother who always motivated and encouraged me. Being a fan of his works and getting inspired every day. Ever charming character of him and adorable writings are the one that inspired me to write this.

Hassain, some persons come into your life and literally shows who you are to yourself. He is such one and still believes in me in whatever I do, more like a brother figure. One of the very few persons whom I discussed this story with. Thank you for the positivity you showed that has driven me here.

Vesly and Dinesh, the ones who always stayed positive in whatever I do. Thanks for involving in discussion and helping this story to attain its best shape.

Janani, the person who first cultivated this idea not today but many years ago also the person behind my pen name. Aswin Saravana, the constant supporter of mine and someone whom loves my success as his.

Muthu anna, who always listened to my stories' first version. Dr. Sowmiya, who helped in clearing some doubts in medical related queries. Ajith Kumar, the one who is politically very clear and a writer who shared pages with me in my first anthology.

Moumita, the compiler of my first two anthologies, the one who believed my writings and helped to make my pen debut. Kishore Kumar.VS, whom we share same political stand. Nagaraj, for keep me focused that we are going to do something. My cousins whom supported me throughout, Meipporul Jeeva, Dr. Kanimozhi Jeeva, Kambar.SM, Thiruvalluvar.SM and Dr. R.Tholkappier. There are so many more friends whom I have to thank for being a well-wisher, some of whom include Samrat Ashok, Madhura Chandran, Bala anna, Ashwin anna, Savithru anna, Vivian, Leslin, Vijay Rahul, Dr. Rashmi Mahesha, Samyuktha, Dhivya Bharathi, Swathi, Sathya, Sathish, Prashanth, Manoj Kumar, Harish, Manoj Christy, Kathir, Aishwarya, Lance Arun anna, Akhil, Kirthiga, Nikhil, Karthikeyan and many more. Kindly apologize me if I missed out some of your names here.

Inspirations and fanaticisms are the ones which makes us to do things we love with more interest and enthusiasm. I have to thank all my favorite authors whom have inspired me through their worlds starting from Jonathan Swift, "The Gulliver's travels" is the first novel I read when I was eight-year-old and instantly started loving the way how reading a book works. I learned how a character sketch should be made from the works of David Baldacci and Agatha Christie, whose characters are going to stay iconic for even several hundred years. The travel journey of a character in a novel also should carry the readers, Paulo Coelho who does this magic anytime if we read, If I can write something about the travel and journey, then I must thank Paul Coelho for being an inspiration and Amarar Kalki for giving

"Ponniyin Selvan." Cecilia Ahern, who aces in blending the emotions with story, I have inspired several moments from her novels and learned how to write about the emotion of a character. Depth of the story is the first hero of any novel; I have realized this after reading James Joyce's "Ulysses" and Mario Puzzo's "The Godfather."

The medium of cinema, which is the easily accessible way to watch stories now, I have grown up watching movies, I bow down to my hero, Charlie Chaplin for showing me that world is a nice place to live and love, through cinema. Next, I sincerely thank these iconic story tellers and filmmakers, Vetri Maaran, Mani Ratnam, Christopher Nolan, J.K. Rowling, Chuck Palahnuik, Martin Scorsese, Quentin Tarantino, Oriol Paulo, Alfred Hitchcock, Steven Speilberg, Gautam Vasudev Menon, Pa. Ranjith, Robert Zemeckis, Lijo Jose Pellissery, Selvaraghavan, Rajkumar Hirani, Mysskin, Karthik Subbaraj, Mahendran, Siddique, Bong Joon Ho, Sanjai Leela Bhansali and many story tellers for inspiring many.

When you write a story, perfection and character developments are the crucial and important part. Vince Gilligan, the creator of TV series "Breaking Bad" inspired me with this. The amount of perfection and carefulness in writing is what I learned from the series, which is Greatest of All Time.

Finally, last but definitely not the least Ulaganayagan Kamal Hassan, the man who inspires me in many ways and his writing tops the all. From his Dasavaratam, I learned how chaos theory plays a role in narrating a story. I took three of his films as a primary inspiration to write this novel. From Hey Ram, I learned how to blend historic and true events to the characters also about how poetic love sequences are to be written. From Virumaandi, I learned what is the basic need of humanity. On the whole, I have learned, what is writing from him.

Special thanks to Madhumitha, Sreedharshana, and the entire crew members of Notion Press publications for making my dream come true.

About The Author

This debut author Porches is an enigmatic youngster, who is full of creative thoughts and interesting stories in his pocket. He was born on 1995 to a beautiful couple in Thanjavur, Tamil Nadu.

He graduated in Mechanical Engineering from J.J College of Engineering and Technology, Trichy. Originally named Porchezhian, he changed his pen name as Porches which is used by his friends to call him shortly, also his social media handles' name. He has a great love towards oceans and hill tops, which reflects in most of his writings.

Porches is known for his creativity, script writing and most importantly critical thinking. He got interested in reading books from the age of eight. His first book was 'Gulliver's Travel' with this his journey towards reading and writing started too.

He has directed six short films from his college days and uploaded in YouTube. Ellam Kadanthu Pogumada (2016), Let's Breakup (2016), Magizhchi (2016), Pallavi Anu Pallavi (2017), Nasayaru Manangetten (2018), Bomma (2020). His short film "Let's Breakup" won the prize in best short film category at Legacy 2016, an intercollege culturals held at Mepco Schlenk Engineering College, Sivakasi, then, "Nasayaru Manangetten" is officially selected and screened at a short film festival at Trichy conducted by Happy theatres.

Also, he is a boy with immense love towards cinema which helped him to earn him the free skill of acting. He makes creative Instagram reels with his acting skills with socially responsible contents in a comic way. He acted in his friends' short films, his recent work is the short film

"Alpha Bravo Charlie" by his friend Vesly Rose, which won third prize in Sathya and Tamil Nadu now's mobile short film contest held at Leela Palace, Chennai. He also involved in open mics and hosted shows.

Although he has been doing everything, his passion and love towards writing never fades. He writes blogs on "wordpress.com," where he took practice towards big stage, he writes short poems and film appreciations mostly and post-match reviews for almost all games of Men's Cricket World Cup in 2019. He is also a voice artist and has released podcasts on several topics and given voice overs for YouTube channels.

When the covid lockdown hit us all in 2020. He started writing short stories, "The first night", "Pslam of life", "It was my fault". He also collaborated in with other authors anthologies. His first published work is "The Mind's Scribble" (2022) by Moumita Adhikary and then he associated with the same compiler for Detour (2022). His stories have unique touch and sweet twists. He also loves Photography, Poems, and Paintings which according to him is "3Ps, The trinity of art."

He claims that his best therapy is reading, stories and papers are the best high-definition screens to watch his dream.

He can be reached at,

porcheswrites@gmail.com
www.instagram.com/ @_porches_
www.facebook.com/ Porches

www.ingramcontent.com/pod-product-compliance
Lightning Source LLC
LaVergne TN
LVHW041215150826
845673LV00001B/409

* 9 7 9 8 8 8 8 1 5 6 7 5 9 *